Black Cat White Paws

A Maggie Dahl Mystery

Mark McNease

Also By Mark McNease

Mysteries
Murder at Pride Lodge
Pride and Perilous
Death in the Headlights
Death by Pride
Kill Switch
Last Room at the Cliff's Edge
Murder at the Paisley Parrot

Audiobooks
Murder at Pride Lodge
Pride and Perilous
Death by Pride
Death in the Headlights
Last Room at the Cliff's Edge
Murder at the Paisley Parrot
Stop the Car

Other Books & Writing
Stop the Car: A Short Story and Kindle Single
The Seer: A Short Story
Rough & Tumble: A Dystopian Love Tragedy
An Unobstructed View: Short Fiction
5 of a Kind: More Short Fiction
Outer Voices Inner Lives: LGBTQ Writers Over 50

Praise for *Last Room at the Cliff's Edge*

"Nathaniel Hawthorne wrote that "easy reading is damn hard writing." McNease writes in this ostensibly effortless way, employing all the elements of a true story teller: intrigue, tension, memorable characters and perfect pacing. I also admire the ease with which he captures a woman's point of view. Linda is heroic and flawed and utterly believable."

Jean Ryan, author of *Survival Skills* and *Lost Sister*
"This suspenseful series launch from McNease (the Kyle Callahan Mysteries) introduces retired homicide detective Linda Sikorsky ... Plausible sleuthing and smart characterizations combine for a winner.

Publishers Weekly

Praise for *The Cat in the Window*
"... truly excellent – New Yorker-worthy, one might say. It was a perfect little Sunday-morning read."

- Michael Craft, author of *Inside Dumont* and *The Mark Manning Mysteries*

Acknowledgments

I'd like to acknowledge the usual suspects: my husband, Frank Murray, without whom my life would be infinitely less fulfilling and whose small house in the New Jersey woods where we now live has inspired me so much.

My fellow author and friend, David Lennon, for his invaluable input on the manuscript and his encouragement in this thing called writing.

My proofreader, Robin Feldman, whose sharp eyes have now read four of my books line by line.

My writer friends whose support keeps me at it, and the many cats who have enriched my life over the decades, from Alice, who I got when I was twelve and who lived an astonishing 26 years, to our two current housemates, Jessica and William. I rely on their company, their annoyance and their purring to let me know that every day with a cat on my pillow is a good day.

And the readers! There wouldn't be any books without you.

Mark

DEDICATION

For Joyce, Carolyn, Carrie, Patty, Dyan, Cathy and Caro.
Sisters make the world go round.

And for Michael Craft, because of cats.

DAY 1

"There are two means of refuge from the miseries of
life—music and cats."

– Albert Schweitzer

CHAPTER One

OCTOBER WAS MAGGIE'S FAVORITE MONTH. The hot, humid air of summer was finally chased away by autumn's chill winds; leaves began to blaze in death, turning red, orange, yellow and brown, as they fell one by one to the ground. For many people, fall was the end of something — the end of their vacations, the end of their visits to family and friends, the end of the slow pace so common in jobs as people took time off and everything came to a halt in the summer bake. But for Maggie, fall, and especially October, was a *beginning*, bringing with its cooler temperatures a sense of renewal and ambition. She always wanted to *do* things in the fall. To accomplish goals she'd been distracted from as she suffered through the summer months. To open the windows and sleep in nature's cool breath. To start over. But now, this year, that starting over came with the cost of immeasurable grief. For this time, at the age of forty-six, living in a large house whose renovation was only half complete, in a town as different from New York City as it could be, she was starting over alone.

Maggie's husband, David Dahl, left her life as unexpectedly and abruptly as he had entered it twenty-four years earlier. They'd met at an art gallery in Manhattan's SoHo neighborhood, at a time before artists and their representatives had moved north and west to the Meatpacking District. Maggie was in the earliest stage of her nonprofit career, working as an administrative assistant at Brooklyn's Hyde Museum of Modern Photography. She'd spent the summer there with an intern named Kate Lennox, an aspiring photographer who would later open her own gallery. The women were still friends, and Maggie had spoken to her several times since David's death, reminiscing on their time together double dating for dinner and a Broadway show or just visiting each other's apartments.

It was at the Schermerhorn Gallery on Mercer Street, a rainy Tuesday in May, when Maggie stood next to a man not much taller than her, gazing at a photograph by a young Japanese-American college student who'd made a splash in the photography world.

Maggie did not remember the student's name. She did not remember much of anything from that night, except going there with Kate and then looking at the photograph, scanning its details left to right, slowly, until she turned and saw him staring at her. The sensation she felt next had been new to her, something electric and almost frightening. Later, when she thought back on it, she could compare it only to something like looking up from the kitchen sink and seeing a face in the window — it had been that startling. But this was not the face of an intruder or a peeping Tom. This was the most handsome, warm, curious, *wanting* face she had ever seen on a man, and he was staring at her!

When he realized she'd seen him, he blushed. She remembered that, too, all these years later, and every day since his death. How *shy* he'd seemed after brazenly eyeing her just a moment before. He'd stepped back slightly, no doubt worried he would alarm her and lose any chance of saying hello.

"I was just looking at this ..." he managed, indicating the framed photograph with a nod of his head, "amazing photograph, it reminds me so much of ..."

"Me," she'd said, looking back at him.

"Pardon me?"

"Me," she'd repeated. "You weren't looking at the photograph. You were looking at *me*."

He'd taken a moment to compose himself, then confessed. "Yes," he'd said, like a boy caught with a cookie in his hand and chocolate on his face. "Yes, I was looking at you. You're even more remarkable than the photograph."

She'd chuckled at that. It was either the clumsiest pick up line she'd heard, or the greatest compliment she would ever be given in her life. And now, with David gone, she knew, as she had known since that rainy night in SoHo, it was the latter: no one would ever make her feel that way again.

She could live with that. She had to. She had a house to finish renovating. A business she'd started with David when they'd moved to Lambertville, New Jersey. A son back in New York City who needed his remaining parent, and a sister coming from Philadelphia to live with her under the pretense of helping her move forward. Maggie knew Gerri had other reasons for leaving Philly, three failed marriages and a recent bankruptcy among them. She couldn't worry about that now. She had to finish getting Gerri's room ready for the move-in that afternoon, as well as go to the small warehouse that served as the production facility for Dahl House Jams and make sure her biggest order to date got out on time. While grief was inescapable, it had to wait its turn on a day like this.

She finished dressing in jeans, a navy blouse and a beige sweater she didn't mind getting dirty, then headed downstairs. She'd thought she heard noises several minutes earlier but dismissed them as the old house settling, something old houses never stopped doing. She was halfway down the stairs when she realized with a start and a gasp that she'd been wrong. It was not the floorboards groaning on their own at all.

"What are you doing in my house?" Maggie said, a half-dozen steps from the main floor.

She could see her entryway clearly, and to her left the large living room it fed into. There in the living room, looking into a fireplace that had not been used in years, was her next door neighbor, Alice Drapier. Maggie had learned early on that some of the locals called the woman standing in her house "Crazy Alice," but she did not like the sound of it or the implications. Having spent her entire life in New York City before moving to Jersey, Maggie had encountered more than a few truly crazy people. Alice was not in that category. Maggie judged Alice to be *eccentric*, which is not the same as being crazy. Alice wandered. Alice sometimes said inappropriate (but never offensive) things to people whose presence she was in. And Alice had the unfortunate habit of intruding where she was not wanted or, in this case, even allowed.

"I've lost Checks," Alice said, bending back up from the fireplace. She'd been staring into the flue as if Checks, who Maggie assumed was one of her seven cats, would come crawling out of the chimney, its tail between its legs in embarrassment, waiting to be forgiven with a treat.

"I'm guessing Checks is a cat," Maggie said. "But that doesn't explain why you're in my house, Alice."

"The door was unlocked," Alice said, as if that justified entering someone else's home.

Alice was somewhere between fifty and sixty. She was short, standing just over five feet tall. She was always in a dress that looked as if it could double for a housecoat, the kind of thing some people called a muumuu, cinched in at the waist with a belt. Her hair was solid gray and her eyes brown, framed by a pair of glasses she kept from losing by hanging them on thin black cord around her neck.

Maggie knew Alice cordially, as many neighbors know one another. She and David had even invited Alice over for dinner once. It was not an experience they'd wanted to repeat. There was nothing bad about it, just that Alice tended to talk nonstop, mostly about her husband Fred who'd been dead for three years, leaving her a house she'd promptly surrendered to cats.

Maggie took a deep breath and continued down the stairs. It was her own fault. She'd left the door unlocked. It was a habit she'd had since they'd moved to Lambertville nine months earlier. There was just something about being able to live in a house with an unlocked door that appealed to her after all those years in Manhattan. If you left your door unlocked there, truly bad things could happen to you. David had told her Lambertville was not some village where everyone knew each other and nothing bad ever happened. It was a fairly large small town, quite cosmopolitan in its way, and it was not safe to leave the door to your house open.

"It's not open," she'd said the first time he discovered it. "It's just unlocked. Nobody would even know that unless they tried the door handle."

"And by then it's too late," he'd said. "No, Maggie, we lock the doors here. Please."

She'd said yes and had kept her promise most of the time, but he was gone now and she just felt like leaving the door unlocked. Now she wished she hadn't.

"Listen, Alice," Maggie said as kindly as possible, stepping down onto the floor and walking up to the woman. "I know how distressed you get when you've lost a cat."

"*Misplaced*," Alice corrected her. "I sometimes misplace them."

It was an odd choice of words. Maggie wanted to tell her that cats most likely misplaced themselves, being independent creatures whose only use for humans was a food bowl.

"Misplaced, then," said Maggie. "I just don't think it's appropriate for you to come into my house, anybody's house, and look around like that. Seriously, Alice, you could get shot."

"Yes, well, I hope not, and I'm sorry, Mrs. Dahl ..."

"Maggie, please."

"Maggie. I apologize. I just worry so much when one of them goes missing."

Maggie had been able to see Alice's cats inside her house next door, sitting in the windows, meandering around. It wasn't a cat house, the sort of place you see on the news after the owner dies and Animal Control finds dozens of cats inside. Alice wasn't like that, and she'd stated the number of felines in her home as seven. That was a lot to most people's thinking, and enough for some neighbors to call the cats' caretaker crazy, but it was not extreme.

"Here," Alice said, taking several folded flyers out of her sweater pocket. Maggie had seen her putting them up in the past when one of her animals had run off. "This is Checks. He's getting old and needs his blood pressure medication."

"Cats have high blood pressure?" Maggie said, taking the flyer.

"Oh yes. Sometimes they go blind from it. Just like people. That's why he needs his pill every day. That's the only reason I would ever walk into your home. It's an emergency."

Maggie doubted Alice needed a life-or-death pet emergency to enter her home uninvited. Alice was known to wander, especially when she was looking for a cat. She didn't seem to think anything of crawling under a hedge row or climbing a fence. Maggie had heard the stories.

She looked at the flyer. BLACK CAT WHITE PAWS, it said across the top in giant black all-caps. Below it was a picture of Checks, who Maggie had seen many times in Alice's front bay window. Below the picture was a description of the missing cat, the information that he needed his medication, and a phone number with a plea to call immediately if the cat was spotted.

"Maybe you can put it up at the store," Alice said.

The store. Jesus, Maggie thought. Another worry for the day. In addition to having a small factory, she and David had planned to open *Dahl House Jams and Specialties* in a small storefront on Union Street. The rent was steep but doable if they could keep the business alive. They'd expected to take a significant loss the first year and had set money aside for it. Then his sudden death, with everything changing. But not his dreams, not *their* dreams. Maggie would not let those die with him—not the company, not the house, not the move to New Jersey. She was determined to stay put and succeed, whatever it took. The store would open before

Halloween, there was no other option as far as Maggie was concerned. That meant days of constant work, work she needed to get to now instead of talking to her addled neighbor who'd taken the liberty of walking into her home.

"The store's not open yet," Maggie said. "Not for another week. I imagine you'll find Checks long before then."

"I have to!" Alice said, startled by the idea her precious Checks could live without her that long.

"Forgive me for rushing but I've got a lot to do today," Maggie said. "My sister Gerri is coming to stay with me, and I've got this huge jam order ..."

"That's an odd name for a woman," Alice said.

Maggie stared at her, her patience having run out. "It's short for Geraldine, not that unusual at all, at least not fifty years ago. Anyway, Alice ..."

"Yes, yes," Alice said, folding the flyers and putting them back in her pocket. "I need to get these put up around town."

"You do that."

"Thank you so much," Alice said, heading to the door with Maggie at her side.

Maggie had no idea what Alice was thanking her for, but she was happy to have the intrusion over. She held the door for Alice, waved at her when she glanced back from the walkway, then closed the door and went about her very busy day.

CHAPTER Two

LAMBERTVILLE, NEW JERSEY, IS A Halloween town. Outsiders, among whom Maggie no longer considered herself, came in droves to view the annual displays put out by everyone with a porch, window or yard large enough to hold a ghoul, without fully understanding the depths to which the townspeople took their frightful passion. They strolled by the houses on Union Street; they drove slowly up and down like teenagers cruising Main Street in small Midwestern towns, gawking at the mummies, witches and zombies in various states of undress on people's lawns and walkways. There was an unmistakable air of competition to it all, each house attempting to outdo its neighbor, but in a playful way. Maggie had come to know enough of these neighbors to realize the competitiveness did not include malice; and, in fact, nearly all the displays were the same from year to year, with just a goblin added here and there or a bloody corpse taken away for repair.

Fortunately, for Maggie, this was her first Halloween living in Lambertville. It did not spur memories from years past. For many people whose loved ones have died, especially spouses, the seasons can bring renewed grief, reminding the survivor of what they'd seen, done and felt the previous year when the other person was still alive. Christmases were notorious for making people think of someone who'd passed away; not so much Halloween. She was glad she had no memories of it with the man whose dreams had brought them here.

Until a year ago, David and Maggie Dahl were diehard New Yorkers. Maggie had lived in New York City her entire life, having been born and raised in Brooklyn before moving to Manhattan just out of college. David had been a transplant to the city, like so many who called it home. He'd grown up in Detroit and moved to the East Coast when he was twenty-five. By the time the two of them decided to move to New Jersey they'd raised a son, Wynn, put him through college, and watched him move to Astoria, Queens. Not exactly far from home, but not the Upper East Side where the Dahls had lived for twenty-three years before agreeing that life outside the city might have more to offer them in their midlife years.

Maggie had worked at museums her entire professional life, beginning as an administrative assistant at the Hyde and working her way up to the Director's position at the Bolyn Museum of Modern Art in Brooklyn Heights. She spent fifteen years there and had expected to someday retire from the job. David had been a successful financial manager, handling the personal wealth of a half dozen very rich clients. He'd been a stock broker before that, and had tried his hand at selling commercial real estate in his twenties. He'd been at the photo gallery the night he met Maggie as a way of prospecting for potential clients. He'd heard the gallery owner was looking to move to a larger space, and he had a few on offer. The gallery owner was not interested; David left the real estate game six months later, and his and Maggie's lives were forever changed by that chance encounter.

previous October they decided to venture out of
⟍ and see what New Jersey had to offer. They
knew the state was beautiful once you got out of the
large cities into the rural counties and towns. It was
called the Garden State for that reason: New Jersey
offers lush valleys, hills, farmland and rivers as far as
the eye can see, once the eye is no longer looking at
Newark Airport or the buildings of Trenton.

They'd been to New Hope, Pennsylvania, once
before and thought it was a lovely town. This time they
headed across the bridge that connects Pennsylvania to
New Jersey and found themselves in Lambertville.
Lambertville. It didn't sound like the vibrant, artistic,
bustling town it was. Much to their surprise, they both
loved it. They strolled for an entire Sunday afternoon,
up and down the streets, looking at the historic homes,
stopping at nearly every shop along Union and Bridge
streets. And while David had said it was a little too
soon to make a definitive judgment, he was smitten
with the place and knew by the time they headed back
to Manhattan that he wanted to live there.

Maggie had been reluctant at first. New York City
was all she'd ever known as a place to live and it took
her awhile to imagine life without the Theater District,
Lincoln Center and Central Park. But she was devoted
to David and she knew he wanted to change their lives.
He'd grown tired of the relentless pace, the demands
and the pressures of being successful in Manhattan.
He'd grown tired of the concrete, the ubiquitous
scaffolding that covered every other building, and the
ceaseless noise. New York City was never truly quiet,
just like it was never completely dark. Not the kind of
darkness you experience on a country road, or out
beneath a blanket of stars. The reflection of Manhattan's

million lights created a permanent gray haze over the city, and David had reached a time in his life when he wanted to look up and see the glowing heavens, when he wanted to lie in bed at night and hear *absolutely nothing*.

"What are we going to do there?" Maggie asked one night when they were reading in bed. It was a habit they'd shared since their wedding night. Both were voracious readers, and each night would end with David holding a book or magazine while Maggie read the next chapter of some historical fiction, her favorite genre.

"Do we need to know that now?" David replied.

They'd met with their financial adviser (David did not think acting as his own adviser, when he handled other people's money for a living, was a good idea) who went over their assets and assured them they would be fine, for several years at least.

"Well," Maggie said, "I enjoy the whole spontaneity of this move, Sweetheart, but there are a few things it would be nice to know before the moving men haul our lives to New Jersey."

"Like?"

"Like, what will Wynn think?"

Their son had been very independent all his life. He was now twenty-two, pursuing a career in freelance journalism and living with his boyfriend across the river.

"He said he was fine with it."

"When we mentioned it as a hypothetical. This is no longer a 'what-if.'"

"He's got Leo. He's got his career. And he hates being mothered."

"This is not mothering."

"Refusing to live your life so you can stay near your son, who wants you to go anyway, is the worst kind of mothering, Maggie. If we stay, he'll know why and he'll feel responsible. It's not fair to him."

Maggie knew he was right but she was still not completely convinced it was a smart move. "So what are we going to do there? We're too young to retire."

"Jams," David said, as if it were the obvious response.

"Excuse me?"

"Jams," he repeated. "We're going to launch Dahl House Jams."

Maggie remembered making a stop on a trip to Maine to see the sprawling property of Kenwood Kitchens, a wildly successful jam, jelly and specialty company started by two women. David had been fascinated by their story and the whole challenge of entrepreneurship, and Maggie remembered him saying at the time they should start Dahl House Jams. She'd laughed it off that day, taking it as a passing comment among the many they shared in their travels. Now she knew he was serious.

"What do we know about making jams?" she asked, closing the book she'd been reading and setting it on the night stand.

"Nothing. That's the point. It's an adventure."

"Which part of it?"

"All of it!" he said, as he tossed his magazine on the floor and rolled toward her. Their twenty-fourth anniversary was coming up soon and they still made love as if they'd been married a week. It was one of the things Maggie held most dear about their marriage, and one of the things she missed most achingly now.

She would never make love with David again. She would never feel him kiss her breasts or glide his finger with a feather's touch along her spine. On the other hand, she would never again wake up to find him dead in his sleep, taken from her by viral myocarditis that had presented as a flu, a bout of heartburn that would be gone in the morning.

Instead it had been David who was gone in the morning. David whose loss cratered her soul and left her struggling to put one foot in front of the other.

She shrugged it off as best she could: the memories, the expectations, the shock. She had not given up. She had not gone running back to New York City in a widow's veil, seeking the comfort of friends who doubted her resolve. No. *Dahl House Jams* was a going concern. They had their biggest order to date, 2,000 jars of custom Halloween jams: Crabby Apple, Strangefruit, and Pumpkin Paradise, a recipe David had been working on when he died. The order would go out on time. The storefront on Union Street would open on time. And, Maggie realized looking at her watch, her sister Gerri would be moving in that afternoon, *on time*. There wasn't a minute to waste, so she guzzled the rest of her coffee, popped a last sliver of rye toast in her mouth and rushed out the door, locking it behind her. She did not want to see Alice Drapier or anyone else standing in her living room unexpectedly again.

CHAPTER Three

THE FACTORY, AS MAGGIE AND her assistant Janice Cleary called it, was a converted auto repair shop a mile outside Lambertville. Located along Route 29 just up the road from a CVS and a popular farmer's market, the building had been empty for several years, though not in disrepair. Its owner, Bud "Auto-Man" Grassley, had died doing what everyone said he loved most: turning a wrench on a car engine, struck down by an aneurism that exploded in his brain.

"He never saw it coming," his wife Maryanne had told Maggie and David when they'd first approached her about buying the old shop. "Like a balloon popping, the doctor said. One second he was under a hood talking to our son Buddy, the next he was gone. I suppose that's a blessing."

Maryanne told them she had not held onto the property for any sentimental reason. It was just that no one had asked to buy it. It wasn't a good location for a restaurant, or a retail shop of any kind. But a factory that made jams and jellies? Why not!

So it was that Dahl House Jams (the official name of the business's jams, jellies and preserves side) made its way from the Dahl's garage into a proper factory setting, and within six months it was running well enough to take on its largest order.

Maggie employed three people besides Janice, making it a very small, tight team that included two local women in their late forties and a man named Peter

Stapley best known around town as the father of a twelve-year-old girl who'd vanished ten years ago. Maggie knew Peter's story. She knew his wife Melissa had left him a year after their child's disappearance, and that he had not been the same since the couple first realized their daughter was never coming home. She did not like to think of herself as taking pity on people (except the demonstrably less fortunate), but there was something about Peter that told her he would not be returning to his old self, whoever that had been. Working at a jam factory was just about his speed at this point in his life and with what he'd endured. The women, Gloria and Sybil, were cousins who'd both returned to the work force after getting their kids off to college. Maggie liked hiring older people. She cared about each of them, and about Janice, the youngest of the crew at thirty-two and the only one who would be dividing her time between the factory and the store Maggie was opening. Janice was her right hand, without whom she might drop every single ball she was juggling.

The morning went smoothly after a slight delay with the jar delivery. Dahl House Jams was a small start-up and Maggie could not afford the kind of equipment she needed to grow the company much more. That was coming, she was sure of it, but for now they made their jams, jellies and preserves by hand, using vats, pots and everything else they needed that David had purchased from a school cafeteria that was upgrading.

The idea for Dahl House Jams had been in David's mind long before their visit to Kenwood Kitchens. His grandmother Patricia used to make her own jams, and one night while they slept soundly in their Upper East

Side co-op, David had a dream about her. According to his retelling the next morning, he didn't remember much of it except that she had served him toast with her homemade jam. He'd been just eight years old when she died. Here she was forty years later, bringing him comfort and bread in a dream. It came back to him on their visit to Maine and the jam company. Then they made the trip to Lambertville. The dominoes soon fell, and now Maggie was a widow struggling to establish a company and open a store in a town she'd only known for nine months.

A few of her friends, the ones who still spent evenings in restaurants on Columbus Avenue or enjoying a concert at Carnegie Hall, had encouraged her to move back. Others carefully suggested the whole thing had been for David, that she had left in pursuit of her husband's dream, not hers. While knowing there was some truth to what they thought, Maggie had no intention of calling it quits and returning to the city. The move, house and business had become both their dreams. She would *not* go running back to Manhattan. She would not give up on the new life they'd just begun when David died. She would not abandon *their* dreams. Not today, not tomorrow, not ever.

Maggie was lost in thought, barely listening to Janice explain the timeline and how they would get the jams made and shipped in the next two days, when her phone vibrated. She kept the sound off, preferring the occasional vibration to having conversations interrupted by a ringtone.

"Excuse me," she said, turning away from Janice. She slipped the phone from her sweater pocket and glanced at the caller ID: Gerri.

"What's up?" Maggie said, stepping away from the small desk where Janice was sitting.

"Where are you?"

"I'm at the factory. Where are *you*?"

"On your front porch! Where I'm supposed to be."

Maggie glanced up at the wall clock. It was 11:00 a.m.

"Three hours from now," Maggie said. "You were supposed to get here around two."

"Yes, well, the movers showed up early and I didn't have as much to bring as I thought. You said I would have two rooms. That's not a lot of space, Maggie."

Maggie sighed. "I meant two rooms for living. A bedroom and an office or whatever you want to do with the second room. But it's a big house, for godsake. You could bring whatever you wanted."

"Which wasn't much. The whole apartment reminded me of John," Gerri said. He was her third and, she swore, last husband, who had left her six months ago for the receptionist in his office, something Gerri had considered pedestrian beyond words.

She'd taken her abandonment as a final humiliation and filed for divorce. "I sold what I could and gave the rest away, Maggie. The furniture, that awful bamboo cabinet from his dead mother."

"He left it?"

"No, he just never came to get it like he promised. I got fifty dollars for it on Craigslist. He said it was worth five hundred, lying prick. Now it's gone, he's gone, and so am I, standing on your porch wondering where you are."

Maggie heard a truck horn in the background.

"They want to get going," Gerri said. "And I'm paying them by the hour. I rode with them, by the way. They smell like movers. Please hurry."

"I'll be there in ten minutes, just hold on," Maggie said. She hung up and walked back over to Janice.

"I'm so sorry …"

"You have to go, I heard. Don't worry about it. I'm on top of it. We all are, Boss. We won't let you down."

Maggie had gotten used to Janice calling her Boss and had stopped telling her not to. She knew that when Janice said they would not let her down, she meant they would not let her *and David* down. He and Maggie had hired each of them. They had grieved his loss together. They'd only known him a month when he died, but they knew him as a kind, funny and generous man.

"Thank you, Janice," Maggie said. "I don't know if I can get back today. I have a feeling my sister is going to suck all the air and time out of me, at least for the day."

"Don't worry! Just go. Call me as often as you need to for reassurance. I'm telling you, Boss, we've got this. You're on your way."

"*We're* on our way," she said. "We're a team, and a good one. This is ours, remember that."

Janice nodded, reached out and squeezed Maggie's hand. Maggie thanked her a final time and headed out of the factory.

CHAPTER Four

MAGGIE'S RELATIONSHIP WITH HER SISTER Geraldine had always been complicated. Gerri, as she'd been called since childhood, was three years older than Maggie and had led a very different life. She'd left their home in Brooklyn when she was only seventeen, running off to be with a man who was ten years her senior and who her parents detested. That misadventure had taken her to Chicago for several years before her husband abruptly left her without explanation. One night he was home, and the next morning he was gone. Gerri never heard from him again and was relieved to be rid of him. She moved back in with her parents while Maggie was in college and living at home, commuting to school by subway. Two more husbands followed, with the third, John Corker, taking Gerri to Philadelphia with him to start a series of failed businesses before he replaced her with his receptionist. Her only regret this time was that it had been so cliché. She would have preferred he run off with a male stripper or rich older widow, *anyone* but a receptionist.

"I think he's gay anyway," Gerri told Maggie one night shortly after John had departed. "The sex was always terrible. Is that a sign?"

"Of being gay, or just a lousy lover?" Maggie had said.

She wanted to feel badly for her sister, but Gerri never seemed to feel badly for herself. It was one of her strong suits: she was a tough one and oblivious to her own misfortune.

"I really don't know what the signs of being gay are," said Maggie. It was just a week before Gerri announced she'd be moving to Lambertville to support her grieving sister, a convenient motive for escaping Philadelphia and the disappointment it represented.

"Wynn's gay," Gerri said. Wynton Dahl, like his aunt Gerri, had always used a diminutive of his name. Maggie and David had never had the slightest issue with their son's sexual orientation; nor had Wynn appeared to have any difficulty with it. He was gay — he knew it from the age of five and Maggie knew it even sooner. She and David cared about Wynn's happiness and the things he wanted to achieve in life, nothing else.

"Gerri," Maggie said, sipping a glass of wine on her couch while her sister, an hour away by car, drank gin, "I don't think there's some list of …"

"Symptoms, just call them symptoms."

"Being gay is not an illness with symptoms, if that's what you're implying."

"*Traditions*, then. Manifestations. Affectations. Whatever. John was dreadful in bed … or on the couch or in the laundry room, wherever we did it."

"The laundry room?"

"It's more common than you think."

They'd shared a laugh at that and changed the subject. A week later Gerri told her she was coming to Lambertville.

"Coming?" Maggie had asked, feeling her stomach drop.

"Moving, Maggie. I'm moving in with you."

Maggie had suspected this was coming but was still startled when Gerri said it so matter-of-factly. "Why would you want to move here, Gerri?"

"Listen to yourself! You're so lost without David you can't even see the obvious. You need me, and I will not, under any circumstances, fail to be there for you."

"You can visit me."

"No, no," Gerri had said with a finality that told Maggie there was no point in resisting, at least not for a while. (She hoped Gerri would find Lambertville stifling, small and inhospitable, and move back to Philadelphia within a few months.) "I will be moving in to support you as only a sister can. You need me, Maggie."

Maggie had wanted to tell her the best way she could help would be to stay in Philly. But ... the truth was she was incredibly lonely without David. The house was so big and empty, more so with the unfinished renovations they'd started. The only company she had anymore were visits from Janice to go over the books, and a local contractor named Chip McGill they'd hired to help with the house. The business was still struggling to finds its legs, and the store was planned for a mid-October opening just a week away. She needed companionship, if not help. She'd not argued with Gerri after that, and now, with things heating up and moving quickly, she welcomed her sister to her home with some appreciation and great hesitation.

The move went smoothly and quickly. Gerri had brought her belongings in a small moving truck, with one man driving while she'd sat pressed between the other and the door. Maggie had hurried home after the call at the factory and found Gerri standing on her porch as if they'd just hung up from talking. The men were sitting in the truck cab smoking cigarettes. One of them glanced at his watch when Maggie arrived, a signal to get this over with.

The entirety of Gerri's possessions consisted of her bedroom set, her clothes, some wall hangings, a filing cabinet, a coffee table, two book shelves, and a desk Maggie recognized as having belonged to their grandmother. Harriet Dahl had been a gossip columnist of minor fame. The desk had been moved into the Dahl home after Harriet died when Maggie was thirteen, and there it had remained until their parents were killed in a car accident on the Taconic State Parkway. A drunk driver going the wrong way had veered into their Taurus and ended their lives instantly. Maggie was forty at the time, Gerri forty-three. The desk was the only thing from their parents' Brooklyn apartment Gerri wanted. Here it was, being moved into Maggie's house and carried upstairs to one of the two rooms Gerri would be calling her own.

The next time Maggie checked her watch it was six o'clock. The afternoon had flown by, with Gerri talking nonstop about her life without "that man," as she called her third ex-husband, about her disillusionment with Philadelphia after living there for so many years, about her expectations for a new life in Lambertville.

Neither woman felt like cooking; besides, Maggie had a habit of keeping almost nothing in her refrigerator. It was another change since David's death: she wasn't hungry and took no pleasure in grocery shopping, the way she had when it was the two of them going aisle to aisle at the Giant in New Hope. Even grocery store aisles seemed haunted to her now, so she avoided the place and shopped instead at a local corner market, buying just what she'd need for a meal of pasta and a salad, or to make a sandwich with a bowl of soup.

"You're too thin, Maggie," Gerri said, when they finally sat in the large, overstuffed matching chairs in the living room.

Maggie and David had brought the chairs from their apartment, where they'd seemed massive and a little cramped for the space. Here, in the Lambertville house David had insisted they buy specifically because it was so large and in need of renovation, the chairs seemed swallowed up by the room. Angled toward each other, they faced a fireplace that had not been used in years and that David had looked forward to lighting logs in. Now Maggie would be doing it alone—or, more precisely, with her sister—but do it she would. Winter was coming, and the room, as well as the rest of the house, had to be heated. Maggie dreaded the bills she'd be seeing.

"I thought you couldn't be too thin or too rich," Maggie said, staring at the cold, empty fireplace, swirling a glass of red wine in her hand.

Gerri looked at her over the rim of her eyeglasses. "I'm serious. You've lost weight, and you were already small as a bird."

Maggie was a short woman and she had always maintained a low weight. It was true she'd lost ten pounds since David's death. On the other hand, she'd finally pulled out of her emotional tailspin and was focused on the factory, store and, soon, the house.

"I'll put the weight back on," Maggie said. "Don't worry about it. You're just thinking about food because you're hungry."

"Well, it's almost seven o'clock. How about DiPalo's?"

Lambertville offered an impressive selection of restaurants, with some of the finest dining in New Jersey. DiPalo's was a local legend, an Italian restaurant run by two women who'd been in business for twenty years and married for five. Maggie knew them well and could think of no better place to eat. But the day had been long, and tomorrow would be even longer as Maggie set about getting everything done before Halloween. Going out to dinner was not something she was really up to.

"How about Chinese?" she said. "There a good place not far from here that delivers."

"Ugh," replied Gerri. Then, probably realizing she'd frustrated her sister, she said, "Sounds fine, Maggie, really. Rice, broccoli, steamed chicken. But *you* get an eggroll and lots of that brown, gooey sauce. You need the calories."

"I'll call them," Maggie said. She was just about to get up from her chair when she heard a noise. She stopped, her hands still pressed on the arm rests. "Did you hear that?"

"Hear what?" Gerri said.

"Shh. Listen."

Both women remained still, turning their heads. Then it was clear: a meowing, coming from outside.

"I didn't know you had a cat," Gerri said.

"I don't. But I know who does."

Maggie got up and went to the front door. Opening it, she saw Checks, the missing cat, perched on her porch just inches from the door. He looked up at her, his expression one of annoyance and impatience. And he meowed. Again and again.

"That's odd," Maggie said, glancing around outside. She flipped on the porch light. Looking down at the black cat with white paws, she said, "What are you doing here, cat? Or should I call you Checks?"

The cat waited silently a moment, as if weighing his response, then yowled, throwing a piercing meow at the woman who did not seem intelligent enough to understand him.

"What's going on?" Gerri called from inside.

"Nothing," Maggie said over her shoulder. "It's just my neighbor's missing cat."

She pondered her options, worried that if she simply closed the door, Checks the cat would keep crying all night.

"I'll be back in a minute," Maggie said. "Get the takeout menu. It's in the kitchen drawer under the phone."

Maggie stepped outside, closing but not shutting the door behind her. She leaned down and picked up the cat. He was heavier than she'd expected, and she had to cradle him like a giant sausage in her arms. To her surprise, he stopped crying and offered no resistance. She hurried over to Alice's house, wanting to be done with the errand and get back for her dinner. She felt mild hunger pangs and realized she may finally be returning to normal, whatever that was.

She rounded the front hedge that gave Alice's house some privacy from the street ... and she stopped, cat in arms. *The lights were off.* That was odd. Despite her habit of wandering, Alice rarely went anywhere at night. She was usually home, and even when she wasn't, she left the lights on, as much for the cats as to foil any intruders. Maggie could normally see lights in the living room and kitchen. If the sun was going down, Alice's lights were coming up, that's how it had been since the first day Maggie and David lived in the house next door.

Maggie felt the cat begin to squirm in her arms.

"Hang on," she said, carrying him up the steps and onto the porch. Holding Checks with one arm, she reached out and rang the doorbell.

Nothing. She rang the doorbell a second time, then a quick third, waiting to see a light come on or a sleepy-eyed Alice open the door and explain that she'd been taking a nap.

No Alice appeared. Instead, Maggie was met with silence and a strange misgiving. She stepped to the side and peered through the front window.

"Oh my God!" she shouted, stepping back and dropping Checks, who landed on his paws and scurried quickly away.

One of Alice's other cats, a fat Calico, had jumped up onto the inner window ledge just as Maggie peered in. The sudden sight of the cat had startled her.

Something felt wrong to Maggie. She cupped her hand over her eyes and peered into the house.

"Huh," she said, stepping back. She doubted anything had happened to Alice, but you never knew. She hadn't expected David to die in his sleep, either, leaving a beloved corpse to shock his wife the next morning.

Maggie decided to go around to the back of the house. She knew Alice had a kitchen entrance there and often used it when she came out to tend her small garden or hang her clothes on a line. That Alice still hung clothes out to dry was another thing her neighbors complained about — this was not a tenement neighborhood on the Lower East Side in the 1930s — but there was no city ordinance against maintaining a clothesline.

Maggie hurried around back, conscious of her sister waiting for her at home. She got to the back door and stopped. It was open slightly. She stared at the door knob. She quickly ran through a couple scenarios in her mind: maybe Alice left the door open hoping Checks would come back; maybe Alice went off to visit someone and didn't want to take her key. *That's absurd,* Maggie thought, still staring at the open door. Alice kept a hidden spare key outside that she'd told Maggie about, in case of emergency; she wouldn't need to leave the door open. She knew the only way she could answer her own questions was to go inside. She reached out and gently pushed the door open.

"Alice?" she called out. "Alice, it's Maggie. Are you here? I found Checks!"

She carefully stepped inside. The kitchen was dark. The whole house seemed to focus its emptiness on this small space, disturbed only by the unseen movement of cats.

The moon provided the only light, sending its faint glow through a window above the sink. Maggie pondered its eerie beauty for just a moment before her gaze scanned down from the window, down from the sink, onto the floor, where she saw it and screamed.

Alice was not gone. Alice was dead, flat on her back with her eyes gray and staring up at nothing. A hammer lay on the floor next to her with what appeared in the moonlight to be a piece of Alice's scalp stuck between its claws.

What if she's not dead? Maggie thought, her mind racing. She hurried to Alice and knelt down, reached for

Alice's arm and felt for a pulse. The flesh was cold. Alice was not breathing. Maggie screamed again.

DAY 2

"In ancient times cats were worshiped as gods; they
have not forgotten this."

– Terry Pratchett

CHAPTER Five

MAGGIE WAS SURPRISED SHE'D SLEPT at all. The last three hours felt like a waking dream broken only by brief periods of blackness. The clock had advanced ten minutes or so each time she'd looked at it before slipping back into oblivion.

"You look awful," Gerri said, standing in Maggie's bedroom doorway. "I've got some coffee for you."

Wearing a thick blue terrycloth robe and holding a large mug of coffee in her hands, Gerri walked over to the bed and set the mug on Maggie's night stand.

"Did you sleep?"

Maggie rubbed her palms over her eyes, stretching the skin of her face. "Here and there, I think."

"It's better than nothing. Are you taking the day off? I think you should."

"I can't, Gerri," Maggie said, picking up the coffee and blowing across the top of it before taking a sip. "The order has to go out soon for Thanksgiving and we're finishing the last batch of Pumpkin Paradise. This is a big deal for us, two thousand jars to Hearth and Home. They've got stores all over the east coast. This could make us, Gerri."

"Can't Janice handle it?"

"She's got enough on her plate. Besides, I need to stay busy."

"David's death still weighing on you?"

Maggie wasn't sure if it was a question or a statement. She said nothing for a moment. She knew grief did not have a beginning, middle and end. One of the best things she'd learned from a bereavement group she'd attended was that "grief is not linear." It's more like a wave that comes and goes. And while she did not want to come out and tell Gerri she was still haunted by David's death, that was the truth. She had trouble most days just moving forward. She knew it would be this way for a long time, but for now she had other excuses.

"It's a horrible thing to find your neighbor dead like that. Murdered, Gerri. Someone smashed her head with a hammer. I can't get that image out of my mind."

"Well, you'll have to relive it for a while at least. You're scheduled to meet with Sergeant Hoyt this morning."

Ah, Maggie thought. *Sergeant Hoyt.* He'd arrived at Alice's house shortly after the first patrol car came. It took only minutes for the police to get there, though it seemed like hours. Maggie was waiting for them in the yard with Gerri standing next to her. She'd led them to the back door. They'd told her to wait outside while they entered the house and saw the body for themselves.

About fifteen minutes later a plainclothes sedan showed up, driven by a man who appeared to be in his early forties. He was wearing a suit with a badge clipped to his belt and, Maggie saw, a gun holstered next to it. He introduced himself as Sergeant Bryan Hoyt and asked Maggie and Gerri to follow him to the front of the house. Apparently one of the arriving police officers had unlocked the door and turned on the living room lights.

The next hour was a blur as Maggie told Hoyt what happened while Gerri waited on the porch at Hoyt's request. Sitting on Alice's couch, listening to the sound of people in the kitchen, Maggie told him how things had unfolded: hearing the cat at the door, taking it back to Alice's house, finding the back door unlocked, and finally seeing Alice's body on the floor with the hammer next to her.

She'd noticed the sergeant glance at her clothes and realized he was probably looking for blood, even as he continued writing down what she told him.

"Did you call the police immediately?" he asked.

"Well ..." Maggie said, feeling rattled and having to stop and think back. "I screamed, and then my sister Gerri came running over."

"The woman on the porch?"

"Yes, she just moved in with me today from Philadelphia." After thinking a moment, she said, "Oh my God, she must have thought I was being attacked!"

"It's okay, Ms. Dahl." Taking her name down had been his first order of business. "Please continue."

"Well, she came running over and I showed her the body, and then we used the kitchen phone to call 911."

He continued to interview her, asking certain questions two or three times. She knew, reflecting on it afterward, this may have been his way of testing her—to see if her story was consistent.

By the time he'd finished his preliminary interview, Maggie knew there were more people in the kitchen with Alice's corpse who had arrived since she'd been in the living room. She could hear them talking as they examined the scene.

At the end of their conversation, Hoyt told Maggie to come to the station the next morning and make a formal statement. He then asked her to wait on the porch while he interviewed Gerri. Impatient and agitated, Maggie had gone home instead, pacing in her kitchen while she waited for her sister to come back. Apparently the sergeant had fewer questions for Gerri, since she showed up at the house fifteen minutes after Maggie had gone home.

Finally, near midnight, they had eaten their boiled eggs and cereal in silence, each tired of talking and wanting to just lie down.

Maggie took another long sip of her coffee and set it back on the nightstand. "You never told me what Hoyt asked you," she said.

"Probably the same questions he asked you."

"Then why was there no request for a second interview with you?"

"Maybe he sees you as the prime suspect and I'm just your alibi."

Maggie looked at her in horror.

"I'm kidding!" Gerri said. "But I am going with you to the station."

"You really don't need to do that."

"I want to be in the room with you when he questions you again."

"Why? And shouldn't I have a lawyer present instead? Oh, God, Gerri, do I need a lawyer? Does he think I killed Alice?"

"Of course not. But let's be honest, he may think you know something about it. Which you don't. This is just how police investigations go."

"How do you know this?" Maggie asked.

"Years and years of police procedurals."

Maggie remembered her sister was a fan of cop shows. Gerri claimed to have seen every episode of *Kojak*, *Cagney & Lacey*, and *Rizolli & Isles*, with seven seasons of *The Closer* thrown in for good measure.

"This is not television," Maggie said. "It's not even reality TV."

"Never mind that. Just get dressed and we'll stop at the police station before we go to the factory."

Maggie had not known Gerri planned to go to work with her but she would welcome the company, and she would politely tell Gerri to stay in whatever waiting area they had at the police station. She'd driven past it many times on the outskirts of town but never had reason to go inside.

"Take your shower," Maggie said. "I'll take mine and we'll stop for breakfast on the way to see Sergeant Hoyt."

"Good," said Gerri. "I'm starving."

She left Maggie alone in the room to finish her coffee. Maggie sipped it slowly, wondering what one wears to an interrogation.

It's not an interrogation, she told herself. *He just wants to ask you ... the same damn questions he asked you last night. Go talk to him. Get it over. You have a life to get on with.*

She set the mug down and headed into her bathroom, slipping off her nightgown as she stepped to the shower.

CHAPTER Six

LAMBERTVILLE'S POLICE DEPARTMENT SITS JUST outside the town proper, along Main Street once it has morphed from New Jersey Highway 29-S. Consisting of several sergeants and a dozen police officers, all supported by a small but dedicated staff, the department serves a community that experiences the types of crimes familiar to a bucolic riverside town— petty theft, burglary, traffic violations and an occasional domestic altercation. Murder is a rarity, and now they had a doozy: Alice Drapler, local eccentric and borderline cat lady, had been found bludgeoned to death on her kitchen floor. The body was discovered by someone new to the community, who admitted to entering the house to tell Alice her cat had come back after running off for the day. At least that's what Maggie Dahl and her sister had told sergeant Bryan Hoyt.

Hoyt met the women in the station lobby. His expression was neutral, neither welcoming them nor displaying any displeasure at seeing them again.

"Can I get you some coffee or water?" he said, offering his hand first to Maggie, then to Gerri, as they got up from their waiting room chairs.

"Thanks, but ..." Maggie started to say.

"We'd love some," Gerri interrupted.

"Black?" said Hoyt.

"That's fine," Maggie replied, wondering why her sister had jumped at the chance for bland office coffee.

Then, to her surprise, he excused himself and disappeared down a hallway. She had not expected a police sergeant to make coffee for visitors. She glanced at the older woman at the front desk who'd asked them to have a seat while she let Sergeant Hoyt know they'd arrived. She did not appear to have any help; perhaps, Maggie thought, everybody pitched in here, including making coffee for suspects.

You're not a suspect, she told herself. *Get a grip, Maggie.*

Hoyt returned a few minutes later, holding a cup of black coffee in each hand. He handed them to the women. Gerri started to sit back down, when Hoyt said, "Oh, please, I'd like to talk to both of you again. I've reserved a conference room."

He led them past the reception desk and down the same hallway he'd used to get their coffee. Maggie looked at Gerri and shrugged. Gerri responded with a self-satisfied smile. Maggie glared at her and the smile vanished.

"Am I a suspect?"

Those were Maggie's first words once she and Gerri had taken seats at the small conference table. Maggie quickly determined it was not an interrogation room, at least not one she'd imagined. The chairs were cushioned and comfortable, not metal and cold. The temperature of the room was moderate, not deliberately high to make a suspect sweat and confess just to get out the room. And there was not a handcuff or leg chain in sight.

"Not at this point," Hoyt assured her.

At what point will I be? Maggie thought. She wanted to ask him that but decided it might seem defensive.

"I will need to record this. You understand."

"We understand," Gerri piped up, with a little too much enthusiasm for Maggie's comfort. The entire thing was happening because a woman was dead; it was not a dinner theater production of a staged murder mystery.

Hoyt reached out and turned on a digital recording device on the table. The days of actual tape were long gone.

"State your name, please."

"Maggie ... Margaret Evelyn Dahl. Forty-six, widow of David Dahl. What else?"

"Do you live at 69 Delevan Street, Lambertville, New Jersey?" Hoyt asked, simultaneously taking written notes in what was either proper shorthand or his own custom scribbles.

"Yes. I've lived there for nine months. Six with my husband and ..." She choked up.

"That's fine, Mrs. Dahl," Hoyt said.

"I moved in yesterday," Gerri added. Her tone was subdued now that she'd seen Maggie's grief resurface.

"Let's talk through this again, step by step," Hoyt said. "Starting when you heard the cat at the door. Then I'd just like to ask ..." He turned to Gerri, not sure how to address her.

"Ms. Lerner," Gerri said. "Or just Gerri. I use my maiden name. I can't imagine going through life with the name of any of my three loser husbands. Who were losers completely on their own, you understand. I had to find out the hard way."

"Thank you, Ms. Lerner. I'll be asking you to tell me your recollections again ..."

"Corroborate," said Gerri.

"Pardon?"

"*Corroborate*," Gerri repeated. "You'll ask me to corroborate what my sister tells you. I'm her alibi."

Maggie's heart sank. She wished her sister had stayed home with her *corroboration* and her *alibi*. She might get them arrested if she kept interrupting.

Hoyt smiled at her. Turning back to Maggie, he said, "Now, you heard a cat at the door."

"Yes," said Maggie, and she began to repeat what she'd told him the night before—what happened, in what order, and how she came to find Alice Drapier dead on the kitchen floor.

Maggie let Gerri drive them from the police station to the factory. Gerri hadn't owned a car her entire time in Philadelphia, choosing to rely on mass transit instead. Driving was one of her pleasures when she had the chance to do it, but Maggie was not convinced her sister was any good at it.

"You have to drive slowly around here," Maggie said, glancing at the speedometer. Many streets in the towns of the Delaware River Valley had posted speed limits of 25 miles an hour or less. There were also those cultish bicyclists who treated the roads as their private Tour de France. Maggie often worried she would come around a blind curve and run one of them down.

Gerri slowed the car. She knew many small towns met their budgets with traffic tickets and summonses. She did not want to contribute involuntarily.

"We told him exactly what happened," Gerri said, responding to a question Maggie had asked her just before telling her to slow down. "You worry too much."

"I have a lot going on. We have to get the order out for Hearth and Home. I need to be at the store this afternoon for a delivery coming in. And now I have a dead neighbor!"

Maggie fell silent, remembering the sight of Alice on the floor. It made her shudder.

"How well did you know her?" Gerri asked.

"Pardon?"

"Your neighbor, Agnes."

"*Alice*," Maggie said, more sharply than she meant to. "Her name was Alice Drapier. And I barely knew her at all. I *saw* her a lot, but we didn't speak much."

She remembered the times she'd heard her neighbors talk about Alice and she felt badly for the dead woman. Having seven cats does not make you crazy. Wandering into other people's homes might qualify, but Maggie thought that fell more under the socially unaware column. Or just oblivious. Alice had struck her as someone who was permanently distracted.

"It was probably a burglary gone wrong," Gerri said.

"That's an understatement. But what would Alice have that anyone would kill her for? And so brutally?"

"Maybe she walked in on him."

"*Him?*"

"It usually is. Him, or them. They work in pairs."

"I'm guessing you saw that on TV."

"I read about it in a newspaper. Home invaders. One knocks at the front door pretending to be a delivery man, the other crawls in an open window, something like that."

"But why kill her?"

"On reflection I think it probably wasn't a home invasion. Most murders are committed by someone the victim knows. Often someone the victim *loves*."

"She was a widow. I think the cats are the only ones she loved."

"But you said you didn't know her. People have secret lives, Maggie. I hate to shock you."

Maggie looked across the car seat. Did Gerri have a secret life? Was she a dominatrix on Tuesdays and Thursdays? Who were the other people in her life, if there were any? She'd inherited some money from their parents, and had done well in two of her divorce settlements. Had she worked all these years? And how, Maggie asked herself, could she possibly not know something so fundamental about her sister?

"Well," Maggie said, "whatever secret life she had died with her."

"Not necessarily."

"What are you talking about?"

They'd pulled into the small factory parking lot. It still looked like an auto body repair shop, which Maggie liked. There were two large garage doors that opened onto the main area where cars had once been hoisted on hydraulic lifts. That was all gone now, but the doors remained, and David had painted them red just before he died. Maggie felt a pang in her chest.

"I'm just saying," Gerri said, stopping the unfamiliar car with a jerk, "we could find out more about Agnes ... I mean *Alice* ... without much trouble."

"If you're suggesting what I think you are, don't. Her house is a crime scene. They've put tape across the doors."

"Haven't you ever gone under a rope before?"

"Put that out of your head," Maggie said, taking her purse from the seat beside her and reaching for the door handle.

Once spoken, the idea was not something Maggie could forget. The more she tried not to think about it, the more it obsessed her. Maybe a little look-see around Alice's house might not be so terrible. She knew Sergeant Hoyt, or others in the police department, would keep her on their list of persons of interest until they had good reason not to. What harm could there be in looking for that reason?

By the time they left the factory, Maggie had convinced herself it would be okay to make a quick inspection of Alice's home. Very fast, very cursory. Alice's killer may have left evidence the police missed, something that could identify him. Maggie owed that much to the woman she'd found murdered on a cold kitchen floor. Or so she told herself.

CHAPTER Seven

MAGGIE AND DAVID CHOSE THE storefront on Union Street partly because it was a main thoroughfare, and partly because Maggie could afford to pay the rent on it for six months while still losing money on the business. That's how long they'd expected to operate in the red with Dahl House Jams and Specialties. Neither of them had owned a business before, but they'd poured themselves into researching the realities of it and believed they could start to turn a profit within a year.

"What if we fail?" Maggie had asked when they first walked into the small empty store that had been a dress shop for several years.

"We won't fail," he'd said. "We have each other no matter what. As long as we're together, we're a success. The rest is a dream, Maggie."

The rest is a dream. David had truly believed that. He hadn't been religious or especially spiritual, but his personal mantra was, *"All things are of the substance of dreams."* He could not attribute the saying to anyone but he told Maggie it was the only thing that made sense to him in a world with so much suffering, violence and sorrow.

"Not all dreams are good dreams," he'd said the very night he died. "But all dreams end."

Maggie heard those words repeating endlessly in her mind over the next three months. Had he known he would not wake up? Had he *sensed* it somehow?

All dreams end ...

"Are you okay?" Gerri asked. They had been at the store for an hour, after leaving the factory and their major order in Janice's capable hands. It would go out that evening, on schedule and carefully inspected by Janice and the others. Every jar, every label, checked over and over. Maggie needed to be at the store to take a delivery of custom designed jam jars and butter dishes. The store would not just be selling Dahl House jams and jellies—they'd added "Specialties" to the name to let customers know they could find much more there: select tableware, custom kitchen items, even homemade potpourri. While they did not want to lose focus on their core product, they knew they could not have a store with only jams in it—they needed an attractive but limited assortment of other items.

"I'm fine," Maggie said, letting the echo of David's voice fade from her mind. She looked at her watch: the order should have arrived by now.

"Can you trace the packages?" Gerri said.

"It's only four o'clock. Let's give it another hour. Cecile promised it would be here today.

Cecile was the woman who owned the foundry in New Hope where the porcelain items were made. She'd become friendly with Maggie since David's death and was planning to attend the store opening next week.

They both turned at the sound of the bell above the front door. David had wanted it there, saying it reminded him of a store he used to visit with his grandmother. Bells above doors were the old fashioned way of letting store keepers know someone had come in.

"Crap," Maggie said. "I meant to put the 'Closed' sign up."

"It's okay," Gerri said, "I'll take care of it."

A woman shut the door behind her, setting the bell off again. "I love that sound," she said.

Maggie smiled at her, recognizing her neighbor Theresa Stanley.

"Tess." Maggie walked toward her with her arms out. The two of them hugged, then clasped hands a moment. "We don't open till next week."

"I know that, Maggie. I just happened to see you inside ..." She glanced at Gerri.

"This is my sister Gerri," Maggie explained. "She moved in with me for the time being. To help get things running, you know."

Tess gave Maggie the sort of pitying look she loathed but had gotten used to since David's death.

"I think that's wonderful, Maggie, just wonderful." Tess looked quickly around the store. "You'll be a huge success, I know you will, and David will be ... would have been so proud of you."

Tess Stanley lived four doors down the street from Maggie. She and her husband Jack often went on long vacations. She would tell her closest neighbors, including Maggie and David, to please keep an eye on the house.

Tess turned back to Maggie. Lowering her voice as if someone might hear her, she said, "It was so awful about Alice, have you heard?"

Maggie stared at her. Clearly Tess did not know that Maggie was the one who'd found Alice's body. Maggie decided not to tell her. Rumor would take care of that soon enough.

"Yes, terrible," Maggie said. She glanced outside, looking for a UPS truck. "Listen, Tess, I'd love to talk but ..."

"I think it was the money," Tess said in an even more conspiratorial tone.

Maggie stopped herself; Gerri came closer.

"What are you talking about? What money?" Maggie asked.

"Well, I am not one to speak ill of the dead ..."

"Of course not," Gerri said.

"And it's not really a judgment," Tess continued. "But Alice was a little strange. Everybody knew that."

"What money?" Maggie repeated.

"Alice was a hoarder," Tess said, as if it were a difficult truth she'd finally spoken. "But not of things or animals, although twelve cats is a little much."

"Seven," said Maggie. "She had seven cats. It's not that many, really."

"One is too many for me," Tess said. "Allergies."

"So what did she hoard?" asked Gerri.

Tess leaned forward. "Money," she said, barely audible.

"Money?" Maggie said. "Who hoards money? What are you saying?"

"I'm saying Alice and her late husband, God rest his soul, did not believe in banks. There are people like that. They don't use computers, they don't trust financial institutions, and these days who can blame them? The belief was ... I won't call it *rumor*, I don't engage in that ... that Alice and her husband kept their savings, which I'm told were considerable after all those years, somewhere in the house."

"And you think she was killed for it?" Maggie said.

"I can't imagine what else it could be. The police have the house taped off, you must have seen that, living right next door."

"We have," said Gerri.

"I'm sure they'll find any money Alice had hidden there, unless, of course, the person who ... you know ..."

"Of course," Maggie said. "I'm sure Sergeant Hoyt ..." She stopped short.

"Who?"

"A sergeant," Maggie said, not wanting Tess to know more than she already did. "From the police department. A friend of a friend. Nothing, really. I'm sure the police will find who did this and we can all sleep better."

"Unless you've got a million dollars hidden in your closet," Tess said.

"A million dollars?" said Gerri, startled.

"I'm just guessing. Maybe it was half that. Maybe fifty thousand, people kill for pennies these days."

"Or maybe there is no money and the whole thing is gossip," said Maggie.

Tess looked slightly hurt. "I don't gossip."

"I know that, Tess. I'm just saying we need to take a deep breath and let the police handle this. If there's money to be found, they'll find it — or whoever took it."

Tess stepped away from them. "I'll get out of your way," she said. "I know you're super busy. I hope those cats are okay."

The cats, Maggie thought. She'd completely forgotten about Alice's cats. She felt a sudden sadness, knowing animal control would have taken them by now. She wondered if they knew Checks needed a pill. That's why Alice had been so upset and wandered into Maggie's house looking for the animal. She made a mental note to find out where they'd been taken and at least make a phone call.

"Listen," Maggie said, "it was so nice to see you. You'll be at the opening?"

"Jack and I would not miss it," Tess said. Maggie had never said more than a few words to Jack Stanley; he seemed like the type who did not appreciate the human currency of small talk.

Tess walked up to Maggie and gave her a quick kiss on the cheek. The move surprised Maggie. Uninvited kisses and hugs were high on her list of dislikes.

They waved at each other as Tess left the store, setting the bell jingling again.

Maggie saw a UPS truck double parking outside.

"The delivery's here," she said.

"I have an idea for us tonight," Gerri said.

"I could use a movie," Maggie said, absently wiping her cheek where Tess had kissed her. "Something funny or ridiculous."

"Oh, this is much better," Gerri said. "We're going treasure hunting."

"What are you talking about?"

"Alice's house. Hoarded money."

Maggie had entertained the thought all day but it now seemed even riskier. What if there was any truth to Tess's talk about hidden money? What if the killer didn't find it and came back? *What if the police were aware of the same rumors ... would they consider the sisters' actions a little harmless breaking-and-entering, or an admission of guilt?*

"It's a bad idea," Maggie said. "We should forget about it."

Gerri shrugged. It was her way of telling Maggie the subject was not closed.

Maggie hurried to the door and opened it as the UPS driver wheeled in a hand truck piled with boxes. She would deal with her sister later. Right now she had a grand opening to prepare for.

CHAPTER Eight

GERRI MADE DINNER THAT EVENING. It was the first time in five years Maggie had enjoyed her sister's cooking. Gerri had just married husband number three then. Maggie and David had hoped it would work out this time for Gerri, but neither had a good impression of John. For starters, he was evasive about what he did for a living. Gerri eventually told them he was an "idea man" and had started several businesses he had to abandon for one reason or another, supplementing his income with money from Gerri's savings.

Through it all—three marriages, two miscarriages, no children, and a life that might make lesser women bitter—Gerri Lerner remained optimistic, assertive, and an excellent cook.

"I'll never use any name but Lerner again," Gerri said as they carried their empty plates to the sink. "No more married names, no more men, except for an occasional hired hand, if you know what I mean."

Maggie raised her eyebrow. "Seriously?"

"Oh, yes. There's an app for that." Gerri laughed.

They'd eaten stuffed sole with spinach and feta cheese Maggie thought rivaled anything from a good Greek restaurant. Garlic mashed potatoes and a beet salad rounded out the meal, with pieces of baklava they'd picked up at Anastos Bakery on the way home.

Maggie quickly rinsed the plates and was putting them into the dishwasher when she glanced up, looking through the kitchen window at Alice's dark, empty house.

Seeing her, Gerri said, "Well?"

Maggie hesitated. "Well, what?"

"How do we get inside Alice's house? Is there a cellar door? Lambertville seems like the kind of place where the houses have cellars."

"Basements. Nobody calls them cellars, unless you're really in the country somewhere and there's a tornado to outrun. I don't know if she has a basement entrance, and it doesn't matter. We're not breaking into her house."

"I don't think taking a look around is the same thing as burgling. We're not going there to steal anything."

Maggie filled the dishwasher compartment with soap, closed the door and started it running. "We're not going there at all."

"Don't you want to clear your name?"

Turning around and staring at her sister, Maggie said, "Clear my name? *Seriously*? There's nothing to clear, Gerri. I haven't been accused of anything."

"But you're a suspect and you know it. You're the one who found the body. Correction … you're the one *they found with the body*. They have to view you as possibly involved."

Maggie leaned back against the sink, thinking about it. "Hypothetically speaking, what is it we would be looking for in Alice's house?"

"Hypothetically? I'd say we could look for places Alice and her husband would hide a half million dollars. Or fifty thousand. What did that woman say? 'People kill for pennies these days.'"

"The whole thing is based on rumor and whispers, some of them malicious."

"Rumor often has a seed of truth at its core."

"That's true. I remember what they said about you in high school."

Gerri ignored her—it was a joke Maggie had told before, based on Gerri's teenage reputation for misadventure.

"Second question," Maggie said, stepping away from the sink. She'd begun to feel trapped against it, as if Gerri were pushing her in, pressuring her to do something she knew was irregular and probably illegal. Still, she thought, a quick look through Alice's house might reveal something important, something the police overlooked. She knew they would be reexamining her story, asking her the same questions they'd already asked her ten times. Maybe there *was* something to find in the house—if not money, then possibly something else that pointed toward the killer. After all …

"There wasn't any blood," Maggie said suddenly.

"Excuse me?" Gerri had moved away, toward the kitchen table, giving Maggie room to pace and think.

"She was bludgeoned to death with the claw end of a hammer." She shivered as she remembered the sight. "There should have been more blood."

"So what? Does that mean anything?"

"It means she wasn't killed there."

Gerri looked at her as if the idea was crazy. "Why would anyone kill her somewhere else and bring the body back?"

"Exactly."

"But we were here all day, Maggie. We would have seen something."

"We weren't here all day. I was at the factory in the morning, and you didn't get here till eleven."

"You're right, I hadn't thought about that."

"Of course I'm right. And that means she was dead on the kitchen floor all day."

"That's gruesome. And sad, lying there dead for hours on the floor."

Maggie thought about those poor cats trapped inside with their deceased owner. The implications of what she'd suggested were clear. "How could it be a burglary gone wrong if she wasn't killed there?"

"I still think the answer is in that house." Then, as if having an epiphany, Gerri said, "What if the body itself was a message?"

"I don't understand."

"Why put her body there if she'd been killed somewhere else? Why not bury her in the woods, or dump her in the river?"

Maggie grimaced at the image.

"Not to be unkind," Gerri quickly added, "but that's what serial killers do."

"Serial killers?" Maggie said, aghast. "So now we've gone from a burglar caught in the act to a serial killer."

"Just hear me out, there's a logic to this. *What if the killer wanted her found that way for a reason?*"

"Of course he did," said Maggie. "He wanted her found in her own home so she wouldn't be found in his. And he wanted it to look like a burglary."

"Or a crime of passion."

Maggie had never considered Alice to be a passionate woman, except when it came to her cats.

"We're getting way off track here, Gerri. The more we fantasize, the farther we'll get from the truth. Stick to what we know: Alice was killed, somewhere, by someone. Her body was brought back to the house."

"Wouldn't one of the neighbors have seen that? How would he get her inside?"

"The hedge," Maggie said. "It provides cover, once he got into the driveway. He'd only have to risk being seen for a few seconds."

Ignoring her, Gerri said, "What if there's a tunnel? Two hundred years ago these old houses had tunnels so they could move around in winter. I've read that."

"You're not listening to me. And I seriously doubt the houses in Lambertville have tunnels."

Maggie turned to the window and stared out into the darkness. She felt a chill on her arms. "This is crazy," she said. "We've talked ourselves into something ridiculous, a lot of made up nonsense. This is how innocent people get accused. I don't like it."

Gerri waited a moment. "So are we going?"

"Of course we are," Maggie replied.

"How do we get in?"

"That's the easy part. Alice kept a hidden key outside, like most people who own a house. And like most people, she told a few trusted neighbors."

"You being one of them."

"Yes. She liked me for some reason. Maybe because I never called her Crazy Alice behind her back. Now get into some jeans and put your sneakers on. Oh, and did you bring winter gloves?"

"Leather, high end. One of John's guilt purchases when he was screwing the receptionist."

"Bring them. We'll be ducking under crime scene tape and making sure we don't leave fingerprints."

"Oh, this is exciting!" Gerri headed out of the kitchen to change.

"It's also criminal," Maggie shouted. She hurried to the kitchen closet where she kept cleaning supplies, Latex gloves, and a flashlight. She wanted them in and out of the house as quickly as possible.

CHAPTER Nine

"WAIT, PLEASE," MAGGIE SAID. SHE knew Gerri was impatient. Her sister had always been the type to run ahead, to risk a fall, to leap blindly into another marriage destined to fail.

They'd entered through the back door, the same way Maggie had gone into the house the night before. This time the door was locked, as Maggie assumed it would be now that the house was a crime scene.

She remembered Alice had shown her the spare key in the window well along the side of the house. Maggie and David were not pet people. They'd never even kept live plants. Maggie hadn't been sure why Alice would trust her with the information, except that they lived next to each other.

"I don't have anyone else," Alice had said. They'd been standing on Maggie's front porch after Alice showed her the hidden key. Maggie barely knew her next door neighbor then and had not invited her in.

"I don't know much about taking care of cats," Maggie had said, assuming that's why Alice wanted her to know where the key was.

"Oh, I wouldn't ask you to do that. I never go anywhere, anyway! I just ... you never know. People fall, they sprain their ankle, that kind of thing. We all need someone who can get into our home in case of an emergency."

Maggie knew she was right. Her son Wynn had a key to the house in Lambertville, just in case. She hadn't known if Alice expected her to reciprocate, which she would not do.

"What about one of the other neighbors?"

Alice had looked down at her shoes, embarrassed by the question.

"They don't ..." she'd said, struggling for words. "They think I'm eccentric."

The neighbors were correct, Alice *was* eccentric. But not in a harmful way, and now, as Maggie and Gerri crept across the kitchen, she felt a pang of regret at not having been kinder to Alice, not having accepted her invitations for morning coffee.

She wondered if she should have told the police about Alice showing up in her living room the morning of her death. All she'd said to Sergeant Hoyt was that she knew the cat was missing and she'd gone over to tell Alice he was back. She made a mental note to tell Hoyt about the encounter.

"Oh my God," Gerri said, gasping and stopping in her tracks. Alice's blood had not been cleaned up. There wasn't much, since a corpse doesn't bleed, but her bloodied hair had created a crimson halo on the white tile. Maggie stared at it a moment, her earlier conviction confirmed: there was no spatter, no brutal spraying of Alice's life force against the cabinets and walls, *because she wasn't killed here.*

"Come on," Gerri said. She'd gotten over her shock and had started moving through the kitchen. She looked back and saw Maggie staring at the floor. "What's wrong?"

"I was right," Maggie said. "She was killed somewhere else ..."

Gerri stopped suddenly at a familiar sound. Both women heard it: the front door opening. It creaked as it swung into the front entryway.

"Somebody's here!" Maggie looked around frantically. Could they get back out without being heard?

"This way," Gerri said. She was pointing at a door next to the stove that led to a basement.

Maggie hurried over and, as quietly as they could, they crept onto the stairs and into the darkness. Maggie gently pulled the door closed behind her, turning the knob in silence as she shut them in.

Sergeant Bryan Hoyt wanted to be alone in the house. This was only his second murder in six years as a sergeant. Homicides were rare in Lambertville but not unheard of: human nature assured that at some point someone was going to kill somebody. It might be a domestic dispute, of which Hoyt had seen his share, or it might be a bar brawl or even a hit and run. Knowing the time would come, he'd kept himself educated in the skills required of an effective investigator.

His previous killing had been a thwarted store robbery, ending with the shopkeeper blowing a large hole in a robber's chest with a shotgun she kept under the cash register. Alice Drapier's death, however, had the makings of something deeply sinister. He'd known when he first saw Alice's body in the kitchen that she had not been killed there. The crime scene techs knew it, too, as would anyone making more than a cursory inspection of the room. There was no blood spatter. There was no sign of a struggle. It was as if Alice had been carried in through the back door and placed on the floor for someone else to find, along with the hammer that had punctured her skull.

He'd heard the rumors about the Drapiers keeping cash in the house and he'd dismissed them as gossip. While theft was a possible motive, the murder had none of the markings he would expect from a burglary gone wrong. At the same time, there was no sense in killing Alice somewhere else and bringing her back just to go through the house looking for money. *Or was there?* Was it possible the killer had forced information he'd wanted from Alice somewhere else and brought her body back to the house? And was she killed for something she had, or for something she knew?

He stood in the living room, glancing around in the darkness. He did not believe in any sixth sense, but he had often come to insights by standing still and listening. It was not spirits that spoke to him, but his own thoughts taking shape.

A moment later he walked to a table lamp and turned it on.

Alice kept a clean and orderly home. There was a couch, old but presentable, facing a large screen television sitting on a TV stand. He'd sat on that couch the night before interviewing the women from next door. There was a matching recliner perpendicular to it, where Hoyt imagined Alice's husband had sat watching sports games or the nightly news year after year. There were photographs and knick-knacks along the ledge of a faux fireplace. And there was cat hair on everything.

The poor cats, he thought. Animal control had come in that morning and taken six cats away. They'd been told there were seven, but one of them must have found its way out of the house, possibly frightened off by the sight and smell of its dead owner on the kitchen floor.

He glanced at a staircase to the second floor and intended to head up later to see what was there. More bedrooms? A mattress stuffed with twenty-dollar bills?

He started to walk into the kitchen for a closer look at where Alice had died, when the cat cried.

"I can't see," Gerri said. They had stopped halfway down the basement stairs while they waited and listened.

"What if it's him?" Maggie whispered.

"Who?"

"*The killer.*"

"That's ridiculous. Murderers don't really return to the scene of the crime."

"Unless they didn't find what they were looking for the first time," said Maggie. "What if he was in the house when I came over last night and it scared him off before he was finished?"

The possibility unnerved Gerri. They had no weapons.

"Get ready to run," Gerri said quietly. She carefully stepped back up the stairs, pulling Maggie with her by the hand.

And then they heard it.

"Oh, crap," Maggie said. She knew the sound well. It's what had started this all. The damn cat was still in the house.

Hoyt heard the animal before he saw it. An impatient, plaintive meow from the kitchen. He walked toward the sound and saw Checks perched in front of a door he guessed led to a basement, crying as if it were lost.

"What's going on, bud?" Hoyt said, staring down at the cat. It was black with white paws, and it was very interested in something behind that door. "What's your name?"

Cats can't talk, so it could not tell the sergeant its name was Checks and that it had no intention of being carried away by animal control, having hidden instead in one of several top secret locations it kept around the house.

The cat cried one more time, then hurried into the living room.

Hoyt stared after it but did not move. The animal had been trying to tell him something, and once it was finished it felt no need to stick around.

Placing his hand within inches of the service pistol holstered on his belt, he turned back to the door and waited, listening. A full minute passed. Finally, easing his palm onto the grip of his gun, he reached out and grasped the door knob with his free hand.

He swung the door open and came face to face with Maggie Dahl and Gerri Lerner. No one shrieked. There were no sudden moves. Just three people in a dead woman's house staring at each other.

CHAPTER Ten

"WHAT ARE YOU DOING HERE?" Hoyt asked.

He was gazing into the stairwell where Maggie and Gerri stood gazing back.

"We could ask you the same thing," Gerri replied.

"No, you can't. I belong here. This is a crime scene. *My* crime scene. And right now you look like criminals to me."

"That's ridiculous!" Gerri cried.

Turning back slightly, Maggie said, "Oh, shut up already. He's right. I told you this was a bad idea."

"Please step off the staircase," Hoyt continued. He moved back, making room for them to come up into the kitchen. "And don't touch anything. You've already contaminated the scene."

"Why would you say that?" Gerri asked.

"Because it's true, Ms. Lerner. I have no idea where you've been in this house, what you've touched … or removed."

"We haven't touched anything!" said Gerri. "We just got here for godsake. And I resent your implication we've removed anything. We're not thieves."

"Oh, pardon me, of course I should take your word on this. Why wouldn't I believe two burglars? That's what you are for the moment. Now let's walk carefully into the living room and have a conversation that's going to determine whether you leave on your own or in the back of a patrol car."

The women stayed silent after hearing they might be arrested. For what, and when, would be determined by their answers to Hoyt's questions. Maggie hoped they could get through this without Gerri saying something foolish or offensive. Her sister had been speaking her mind all her life, sometimes with disastrous results and three times to divorce attorneys.

Hoyt let them walk in front of him as they went into the living room. He remained standing while Maggie and Gerri took seats on the couch.

"Now," Hoyt said, giving them a moment to compose themselves, "how did you get into the house?"

"I have a key," said Maggie. "Actually, it wasn't in my possession, but Alice told me where she kept it. A lot of homeowners keep keys outside in case they get locked out."

"Are you a homeowner, Sergeant Hoyt?" Gerri asked, feigning sweetness.

Hoyt ignored her. "I'll be taking that key when we're finished here. Now tell me *why* you're in the house. Keep in mind how it looks, and tell me the truth."

Maggie thought a moment. She knew lying was not an option and would only get them deeper into trouble. She took a breath and said, "I … *we* wanted to see if there was anything here that might give an indication of why Alice was killed, maybe even who killed her."

"Was there a starting point for this little excursion? Or did you just plan to look through everything and see if the person responsible for Alice Drapier's death left a written confession in a drawer somewhere?"

"We were looking for the money," Gerri blurted.

Maggie felt her hopes sink. Her sister had just made things worse: now they would look like robbers as well as murderers.

"Let me explain," Maggie said.

"Please do."

"People talk, Sergeant, as you know."

"Do I?"

"It's a small town, or not a very big one. I didn't know Alice well, but I'd heard things about her. I never called her 'Crazy Alice,' by the way."

"That's kind of you."

"We were at the store this afternoon and someone came in."

"She forgot to put the Closed sign up," Gerri added, as if it were a telling detail.

"She knew from the rumor mill that Alice was dead, and she said something about money ... apparently there's long been gossip about the Drapiers keeping cash in the house. And we thought ..."

"What a perfect motive for murder?" said Hoyt. "Did you think the perpetrator left the money in the house?"

"I don't know what I thought," Maggie said, frustrated. "I just believed that Alice was killed for some reason other than being in the wrong place at the wrong time. I knew you'd think I could have something to do with it—I'm the one who found her dead. And we just thought we might uncover some clue about the whole thing."

Hoyt waited a moment, then asked, "Why do you think she wasn't in the wrong place at the wrong time?"

"Because she wasn't killed here," Gerri said.

"Really? And how do you know that?"

"Sergeant," Maggie said carefully. "I could tell last night from looking around the kitchen that she wasn't beaten to death there. It took a while to register, but then it hit me. There was no blood anywhere but where her head was, no signs of an attack."

"So you're a detective now."

"Not at all. Listen, it was a difficult day all the way around, starting with Alice wandering into my house looking for her damn cat."

Hoyt looked surprised by the new information. "She wandered into your house? What does that mean?"

"I came downstairs yesterday morning ..."

"I wasn't here yet," Gerri said. "I was still in Philadelphia waiting for the movers."

"Anyway," said Maggie, impatient with her sister's interruption, "I had the bad habit of not locking the front door. David was always on me about that, but after so many years in New York City I just ... I don't know ... I wanted to think I lived in a place where you can leave your door unlocked."

She waited a moment, expecting Hoyt to comment. When he didn't, she said, "I came downstairs and Alice was standing in my living room, looking around. I confronted her about it, nicely, and she said she was looking for her cat. The same cat that got me over here last night."

"And told you we were in the basement," Gerri added, apparently blaming the cat for everything.

"So," said Hoyt, "not only did you find her dead, but you may have been the last person to see her alive, apart from whoever attacked her."

Maggie felt her stomach tighten. Things were quickly going from bad to worse. "I sent Alice on her way and went about my business. That was the last I saw of her until I found her in the kitchen last night and called the police."

Hoyt stood there looking at them. "Was that something she'd done before, walk into your house uninvited?"

"No, not my house specifically, but it was something she was known for," said Maggie. "I suppose that's why they called her Crazy Alice behind her back, that and having seven cats."

Maggie could see Hoyt thinking about what she'd said. She wondered if he was making the same educated guess she was: that Alice Drapier's habit of going where she was not wanted or expected had contributed to her sudden death.

"I have the authority to arrest you," Hoyt said, "and I could charge you with breaking and entering."

"We had a key!" protested Maggie.

Ignoring her, Hoyt continued. "But I'm going to let you go. I think you're more inept than anything—"

"Well," sniffed Gerri.

"—and I have things to do, obviously. For now I'm going to take the two of you at your word and reserve judgment."

"Thank you so much," Gerri said, quickly standing up.

"Wait just a moment. I will not forget finding you here. You're technically and legally intruders, even if you used a key. I'm letting you go for my own benefit— I don't need the distraction of filling out paperwork over this. Finding a murderer is my priority and as much as I'd like to close the case, I don't think either of you are the type to bludgeon someone do death. I could be wrong. But you did help in a blundering way."

Maggie could see Gerri was about to protest again, offended at being treated like misbehaving schoolgirls. She clenched her jaw and glared at her, silencing whatever her sister was about to say.

"For all we know the person who killed Mrs. Drapier knew where that key was, too," Hoyt said. "I'm going to want to question both of you again."

"Whenever you need to," Maggie said. She was anxious to get out of the house.

"I'll take that key now." Hoyt pulled a small evidence bag out of his jacket pocket and held it open.

Realizing her fingerprints were on it, and that the killer's might be too, Maggie gently pulled the key from her pants pocket and dropped in into the bag.

"Through the front door, please," Hoyt said.

He walked them to the door and opened it. Yellow crime scene tape was draped loosely in a diagonal across the open frame. He carefully stepped under it, motioning for the women to follow.

Maggie did not look back as they walked quickly across Alice's lawn. She didn't need to: she felt him staring at them all way the back to the house.

CHAPTER Eleven

"THAT WAS A CLOSE CALL," Gerri said. "And a warning. The police know what they're doing, let them do it."

They were in the kitchen, Gerri sitting at the table while Maggie walked repeatedly between the stove and a storage cabinet.

"What are you looking for? You've gone back and forth three times now."

"I don't know," said Maggie. "I thought of having coffee but it's too late. I'd never get to sleep. I might not anyway."

"Are you hungry? I can make you some soup."

"God no. Food is the furthest thing from my mind." Turning to Gerri, she said, "Do you think we're being watched? I had the strangest feeling ..."

"Watched by who?"

"I don't know. The police, certainly. He let us go just now, Gerri. Is that natural? Maybe he let us leave because he has backup, you know, someone parked outside the house."

"Of course. They've tapped the phones, and a crime unit moved into the house across the street and set up a telescope. They're staring at us right now."

Maggie leaned over the sink and peered out the window.

"Oh, for chrissake! We're not being watched. He let us come home because he knows we had nothing to do with it. Besides, he told us he didn't want the hassle.

They have to fill out a dozen forms when they arrest people. It would just be a huge waste of his time. What do you think of him, by the way?"

Maggie stepped back from the sink and looked at her sister. "How do you mean? Are you asking if I think he's good at his job?"

"I mean, don't you think he's attractive?"

"Seriously? We just barely escaped being arrested for burglary and you're fantasizing about the guy?"

"It's been awhile."

"I'd say so. I would also point out that he's at least ten years younger than you are."

"That never stopped me."

Maggie's eyebrows shot up. She knew she shouldn't be surprised that her sister had a sex life, it just wasn't something they'd ever discussed.

"You're remarkably flippant."

"I'm not flippant at all," said Gerri.

"*Unserious*, then."

"You know, Maggie, I think it's time to go to bed. I might say something you don't approve of and I'd rather not end the night like that."

"I agree. I'm tired, too. If I lie down, my mind will stop racing eventually. And I didn't mean to upset you. I just want you to acknowledge the gravity of the situation. Sergeant Hoyt let us go tonight because it suited him. That may not always be the case."

Gerri was getting up from the table when the sound came again. *That* sound. The cat's meow that was now familiar to them both.

"Oh, Jesus," Gerri said. "Not that damn cat again."

They both stood in silence, waiting for the cat to stop crying. It did not.

"He wants in," Maggie said.

"Don't let him."

"But he'll just sit outside the front door and cry all night."

"Use ear plugs."

"I don't have ear plugs." Maggie made a decision. "I'll let him inside, just for the night."

"That's what I said about my last husband when we met. Listen, Maggie, I'm going upstairs. You do what you have to, but if that cat cries all night I'm putting it in the basement."

They left the kitchen. Gerri headed upstairs while Maggie went to the front door and opened it.

Checks stopped meowing and looked up at her. Maggie had the feeling his plan had succeeded and he knew it. Staring down at him, she remembered he needed medication for high blood pressure. She'd thought it was an odd thing for a cat to need when Alice had said it.

He didn't budge. "Well," Maggie said, stepping aside. "Come in, then. You can stay for the night. Tomorrow I'm taking you to a vet—I can at least do that for poor Alice—but you're not coming back here, you understand me? I'm not a cat person. I'm not a *pet* person. I don't even have plants, so don't get any ideas. What do you eat, by the way?"

Checks sauntered into the entryway and waited.

"Fine, I get it," said Maggie. "You won."

She headed back into the kitchen with Checks close behind. "I've got some tuna, I hope that suits you. Otherwise you're out of luck."

She discovered minutes later that tuna suited the animal very well. He gobbled it up from a small bowl on the floor while Maggie went upstairs to try and sleep.

David always looked the same in Maggie's dreams: 47, handsome, thin, with a self-assured smile he'd often used to get his way. Like when he wanted to uproot them and move to Lambertville. He'd assured her there was nothing to worry about, they had the financial resources, and they had each other. Everything else would sort itself out.

"So what are you going to do?" he said. He was sitting naked on the edge of the bed. He'd always slept that way, even when Wynn was a child and known to come bursting into their bedroom uninvited. He had always been comfortable in his nakedness, unlike Maggie who slept in a nightgown.

She sat up and stared at his back. It was another of her lucid dreams — those dreams in which she *knew* she was dreaming, but could not control it.

She mouthed her words, unable to get them past her lips with any sound.

"What *are* you saying?" he said over his shoulder.

She tried again, making no sound or sense. Finally she slapped her chest in frustration and managed to shout, "Do about what? ... What, David, do you want me to do something *about*? About *this*?" She indicated the bedroom, his naked presence in it. "I can't do anything about it. You're dead. You're sitting on our bed. You're asking me what I'm going to do about something without telling me what that something is."

He turned further toward her, twisting at the waist. "The dead woman, of course. Alice Whatshername. I'm glad we were nice to her, I'll say that."

Maggie let herself fall back on the mattress. "Oh for godsake, David. I can't do anything about it. It's enough

71

her cat has moved in for the night. Tomorrow it's out of here. I won't have two more beings in this house, Gerri's more than enough."

"You owe it to her—"

"*Excuse* me?" she said, cutting him off. "I *owe* her finding out who killed her? I don't think so, David. And don't smile at me like that, it was always infuriating … well, not always, only when I knew you were trying to get your way with it. No, I don't owe Alice anything."

"He wanted you to find her."

She stared at him. Surely he didn't mean the killer had wanted her to find Alice's body. "Who are you talking about?"

"The cat, of course. He came over here crying because he wanted you to find her."

"That's crazy."

"Is it?" he said, before turning back around, facing away from her again.

She felt herself reaching out, wanting desperately to touch his back, to feel his skin on the tips of her fingers.

"He knows, Maggie, and he's trying to tell you."

"Knows *what*? That he's hungry? That's about all cats know, and when it's time for a nap."

"He knows who killed her, but you see … " He turned back around for a last look at her. "Cats can't talk. They can't open doors. They can't ask questions." And then, that infuriating, amazing, heart-melting smile. "That's what he expects you to do."

David began to fade, growing fainter with each effort Maggie made to reach her arm to him. She was mute again, trying to speak, to say how hard her days and nights were without him. He knew that, didn't he? Wherever he'd gone, if only out into the universe, he knew how much she missed him … he had to.

She woke up suddenly, and she knew it was the real world, the waking world. The dream had been almost as vivid as the darkness she now peered into.

She pulled back quickly, startled by a shape not two feet in front of her. Checks was sitting on David's pillow, purring.

Maggie reached out and stroked him, which only made the purring more insistent.

He stared at her a moment, then licked her hand.

"You're as manipulative as he was," she said, petting him with the hand he'd just scraped with his tongue. "Fine, then. I'll ask questions and open doors if I can find them. But you're going to owe me, cat, you hear that?"

He seemed satisfied by Maggie's promise; he curled into a ball on the pillow and rested his head on a paw, letting his eyes close.

I should be so lucky, Maggie thought. Sleep would not be coming for her again that night. She glanced at the bedside clock, relieved to see it was almost 4:00 a.m. Early, but not so early she couldn't get up in another half hour and have coffee. Starting the day had always been better than lying in the dark thinking about it.

DAY 3

"Cats know how to obtain food without labor, shelter without confinement, and love without penalties."

– Walter Lionel George

CHAPTER Twelve

THERE WERE TWO VETS IN Lambertville. One of them was far enough to require driving. Maggie made an educated guess that Alice would not have taken her cats to the furthest one. She had a car that sat in a detached garage behind the house; Maggie had seen her drive it only once and had wondered if anyone would come to take it away now that Alice was dead.

She made her first call to Bridge Street Animal Hospital, the vet's office she could walk to, and her guess proved correct. She told the woman who answered the phone that she had an unusual situation — she needed to bring in someone else's cat but wasn't sure if this was the right place.

"What would the patient's name be?" the woman said with professional cheer.

"The patient?" asked Maggie.

"The cat."

Oh, Maggie thought, *of course they call them "patients."*

"Checks," she said.

"Like the cereal?"

"I don't know, actually."

"What is his last name? Or hers?"

"It's a he, and his last name is Drapier."

There was prolonged silence on the other end of the line and Maggie wondered for a moment if she'd been put on hold. Finally the woman said, "That's Alice Drapier's cat. The *late* Alice Drapier. Who is this?"

Maggie felt a strange guilt, as if she'd been caught doing something wrong. "I'm Alice's next door neighbor."

A gasp. "The one who found her dead?"

The call was not going as Maggie had hoped. She wondered if word could spread any faster than it already had. "Yes, that's me. I don't know what happened to Alice's other cats, but one of them is now in my possession and Alice had told me he needs medicine."

As if it had all suddenly fallen into place, the woman said, "Oh! *That* Checks! Of course, I know him well. Everyone in the office knows Checks."

Well, thought Maggie, she'd met an animal whose reputation preceded him. "I'd like to bring him in. He needs a pill or something, I don't know. Alice said he had high blood pressure."

"Oh my gosh," the woman said. "Yes, yes, bring him in as soon as possible. That's a life threatening condition. I should know, I have high blood pressure myself. What did you say your name was?"

"I assumed you knew," Maggie said dryly. Given how much the recent events had been gossiped about throughout town she wouldn't be surprised if everyone knew her name by now.

"Why would I know your name?"

"Never mind. My name is Maggie Dahl. Can I bring him in at ten?" That gave her an hour to rally Gerri, get Checks off the bed and take the first trip of her life to a veterinarian's office.

"Lucky you, we just had a cancellation at ten."

"Lucky me," Maggie said. "We'll see you then."

Maggie and Gerri stared at Checks while he ate some crushed-up granola from the same bowl he'd eaten from the night before.

"Do you think it's safe?" Gerri asked. She'd been up for two hours but had stayed in the seclusion of her room until Maggie shouted for her to get a move on. "I've never heard of cats eating granola before. He seems to like it."

"I'm sure he would tell us if he didn't," Maggie said. She had already concluded this was no ordinary cat. "The bigger question is how we get him to the vet's. I don't have a cat box."

"Speaking of which ..."

"I know, cat litter, I can't worry about it now. We'll get this taken care of and bribe them to keep him. They can worry about cat litter. I'm talking about what we carry him in from here to there."

Checks stopped eating, turned and looked up at them, as if he knew they were talking about him.

"How about a towel?"

Maggie thought about it. She didn't want to put him in a cardboard box; he could just jump out of it and she certainly wouldn't close the lid. A towel might be her only option. She stared at Gerri, not saying anything for a moment.

"Don't look at me! I'll drive if you'd like, but I'm not carrying a cat. Besides, Maggie, he likes you."

"Please don't say that." Turning slightly so Checks wouldn't hear her, she whispered, "He's not coming back. I don't want him to like me. Now let's go, it's nine forty-five."

Although the vet was within walking distance, Maggie was not about to carry a cat for six blocks. Instead she had let Gerri drive while she held Checks in her arms—he had eschewed the towel and insisted on riding in her lap. She suspected this was a deliberate move on his part.

They parked a half block from the vet's office and Maggie carried Checks to the door, feeling foolish and hoping they wouldn't be seen by anyone. She knew people loved to fawn over babies and animals. If anyone stopped her to say how adorable it was carrying a cat in her arms, she worried she would throw him at them.

Gerri held the door open while Maggie entered the vet's office. A chorus of dog yelps greeted them, along with several nervous cat owners sliding their cat carriers between their protective feet.

"Oh, Jesus," said Maggie. She feared Checks would bolt, but he just stayed in her arms and stared down a terrier and a Great Dane. They might tear Maggie to pieces but they were no match for Checks.

She hurried to the front desk. There was movement in the hallway beyond, where doctors examined furry patients. Two women were behind the desk, one facing a side credenza and the other facing clients. When she looked up, Maggie saw the woman's left eye was glass and slightly misaligned. It startled her for an instant; she quickly regained her composure and noticed herself shaking Checks slightly in her arms, the way you shake a baby gently up and down. She stopped.

"You must be Maggie," the woman said. "I'm Susan, and that is Checks."

"You've met."

"Many times." Then, to the cat, "Haven't we, sweetheart?"

Does anyone know what they're getting into with this cat? Maggie thought.

"I'm sorry," she said. "I didn't have a cat box, or carrier, whatever you call them."

"Oh, he doesn't need one. Do you, big boy?"

"How long is this going to take?"

"Just have a seat, please. Dr. Ramsey will be with you in a few minutes."

Maggie turned around to see where Gerri was and saw her already sitting along a row of chairs. A woman with a cat carrier was two seats to her left, and someone holding a poodle in his lap was to her right. Gerri patted the empty seat between herself and the woman. Maggie shuffled over, sitting down with Checks held firmly in her arms. Susan the Desk Clerk may not think he needed the protection of a carrier but the Great Dane didn't look so sure.

Dr. Emily Ramsey had better bedside manners than most human doctors Maggie had met. Diminutive even by the standards of short people, she was pleasantly pudgy and wore her waist-length gray hair tied back with yellow yarn.

Maggie had left Gerri in the waiting area while she brought Checks back to examination room #3. She'd never been in a room like this before and wasn't sure what to do other than set Checks down on the stainless steel counter and hope he didn't make a run for it. *That's a stupid thought,* she'd told herself while she waited for the doctor to come in. *This cat doesn't run from anything.* Seconds later the doctor arrived and greeted Checks with a smile and a "Hey, Sweety!" before introducing herself to Maggie.

"It was terrible, what happened to Alice," the vet said. She slowly petted Checks with one hand while she looked into his ears. "I understand you're the one who found her."

Oh, for chrissake, Maggie thought. *Is there anyone in Lambertville who doesn't know this by now?*

"Yes, I am," she replied. Quickly changing the subject, she added, "Unfortunately this cat—"

"Checks."

"Right, of course you know his name."

"Checks is famous."

"I'm discovering that. I'm also told he takes medication for high blood pressure. And now he's an orphan."

Dr. Ramsey smiled at her. "Not for long."

"Pardon?"

"I'll get a new prescription for you." She gave Checks a last affectionate pet along his spine. "He needs one pill every morning. You can put it in a flavored pill pocket. If you don't have any we've got some samples."

"But I ... he's not ..."

"You can pay up front," Ramsey said. Then she turned around and left through the room's back door, heading into whatever constituted the innards of a veterinarian's office.

"Just like that?" Maggie said, staring at the closed door.

As if knowing he had to seal the deal immediately, Checks walked the few steps on the steel counter and starting rubbing against Maggie. The sound of his purring filled the room.

"Oh, hell no," Maggie said. "No, no, no."

Susan slipped the pill bottle into a small pharmacy bag and placed it on the counter along with a sample of chicken flavored pill pockets.

"Do you know how to use these?" she said.

"I can guess," said Maggie, once again holding Checks in her arms. Gerri was standing behind her. Maggie could swear she felt Gerri's I-told-you-so smile boring into her back. "I don't suppose you have any spare cat carriers and litter boxes?"

"Sorry, no," said Susan. "But Pets Galore has anything you need. They're three doors down."

"Great. That's our next stop."

Maggie had considered asking if they could just leave Checks there, or if the vet's office could find someone to adopt him, but something had stirred in her while she'd been in the examination room. She didn't know if it was David's ghost, or Alice's, or if the two of them were in cahoots from some afterlife surveillance state, but she had decided to take Checks home—to nurse him back to health, although his condition would be lifelong, or to foster him ... isn't that the word they used for animals, too? ... until she could find a good home for him. What she could not accept herself doing was abandoning him at a vet's office. She had no idea where Alice's other cats went and preferred not knowing.

"How much do I owe you?" Maggie said.

"Well," said Susan. She hesitated, then looked around to make sure her office companion was not sitting beside her and none of the pet owners could hear her.

"I wanted to ask you about that."

Maggie leaned forward, aware that Susan meant this as a private conversation in a public setting. "Ask me about what?"

"Alice's outstanding bill. She had *seven* cats."

She also had a half million dollars hidden in her house, thought Maggie. "So how much is this bill?"

"Eight hundred and thirty-seven dollars."

Maggie stared at her. "Seriously?"

Lowering her voice even more, Susan said, "Poor Alice. She had problems ..."

"She also owned a house, and, I'm assuming, a bank account."

Susan looked around again to make sure no one was listening. "No, I mean *problems*. A gambling problem. She was very in debt. She wasn't working, and the bank wouldn't give her a second mortgage. We were friends, Mrs. Dahl. But I couldn't help her. I'm part time here and that's my only income."

"I'm sorry," Maggie said, not sure if that was the proper response. "How did Alice get into debt?"

Susan sighed. "She liked her bus trips to Atlantic City."

Maggie was stunned. She would never have imagined Alice Drapier going off to be a high roller at the penny slots. She'd seen Alice heading off plenty of times, but had always assumed she was walking into town or across the bridge, not to a bus stop for a trip to Atlantic City.

"I went with her a few times on the charter bus. Old people mostly, not what you imagine serious gamblers to look like. It was fun at first, but her ... *addiction* ... I don't know what else to call it, it was too hard to watch. At the craps table."

"The craps table!" Maggie blurted.

Now people were paying attention.

Hurrying, Susan said, "She owed someone money, that's all I know. A *lot* of money."

"You need to tell the police."

Susan began quickly shuffling papers on her desk. Her confession had come to an end. "I can't get involved. I don't know who she got her gambling money from. But it wasn't a *bank*."

The other office assistant came out from the hallway leading behind the examination rooms. "Sorry to take so long," she said to Susan. "My tummy's not in good shape today."

"No problem," said Susan.

Another vet came out, an elderly man Maggie had not seen in the thirty minutes they'd been there. It was clear Susan had divulged whatever she could and would not say more.

"Here," Maggie said, fishing out a credit card with her free hand. "Put it all on this."

"Thank you," Susan said. "Thank you very much."

"Can we go now?" Gerri asked.

She'd been standing directly behind Maggie and the sound of her voice came as a shock. Maggie turned her head enough to see her sister.

"I heard it all," Gerri said. "Now let's get the hell out of here."

Maggie signed the credit card receipt, smiled at Susan a last time, and followed Gerri back out onto the street.

"The car's this way," Gerri said when Maggie turned left on the sidewalk, heading in the opposite direction.

"I know that. There's a pet store we need to go to first. And don't say a word, not one word."

She headed up the street with Checks in her arms, looking for the sign to Pets Galore. Gerri hurried behind her, barely containing her amusement.

CHAPTER Thirteen

MAGGIE WAS GLAD TO BE home with Checks, whom she would now make an effort to call by his name rather than referring to him as "the cat." He was hers now, and she was his. She felt it with reluctant pleasure. She had to admit to herself that with David gone and their son Wynn well into adulthood and happily living his own life, she missed belonging to someone. Her sister didn't count.

"Are you going to rename him?" Gerri asked.

They'd just arrived home with Checks, a large bag of dry cat foot, a dozen cans of wet food, a bag of litter and a large litter box. Maggie was holding the litter box in her hands, standing in the kitchen trying to figure out where to put it.

"Why would I change his name?"

"He's your cat now. You can name him anything you want."

"He's nobody's cat. And he's old. Ten, according to his chart at the vet's."

"They have charts? Like people?"

Maggie stared at her. "No, Gerri, they keep the medical records on index cards. *Of course* they have charts. Now where should we put this?" She held up the litter box.

"Outside, definitely."

Maggie made a face. "Winter's coming. No, I'll put it in the bathroom. I think that's the usual place."

"But we go to the bathroom in there!"

"Listen to yourself," Maggie said. She headed toward the bathroom, with Gerri following behind.

As they were walking down the hallway the doorbell rang. Maggie stopped and turned toward the sound. "Oh, shoot, I forgot."

"Your boyfriend's here?" said Gerri. "Should I hurry upstairs and hide?"

Maggie glared at her. It was much too soon to joke with her about boyfriends, dates, or sex.

"Sorry," Gerri said.

"Don't worry about it. And don't bring it up again, please. This is Chip McGill. He's working on the house for us ... for me. We're renovating. *I'm* renovating."

"It's okay," Gerri said, "with the words—past tense, present tense, 'I' and 'us.' It's going to take time."

"Here," said Maggie, handing the litter box to Gerri. "Put it on the side of the toilet and fill it with litter, I'll let Chip in."

Gerri took the box and kept going toward the bathroom while Maggie walked to the front door.

Chip McGill was a local handyman and carpenter with a reputation both good and bad—good because when he worked, he did an excellent job; bad because he'd been an active alcoholic for years and was known to experience work stoppages due to binges and severe hangovers.

At forty-eight, he looked a good ten years older. He was thin from a diet consisting of cheap whiskey and an occasional meal. His hair was prematurely and completely gray, and appeared to be seldom washed. There was a dark leathery cast to his skin year round, and his eyes were rheumy. He was, by all accounts, a good man, just a damaged one, and the locals were known to give him work as much from a sense of charity as from needing a good contractor.

"Hey, Mrs. Dahl," he said when Maggie opened the door. He was wearing his usual white overalls spattered with paint and putty.

"Morning, Chip. I almost forgot you were coming."

"I can come back later," he said.

"No, please, come in."

She stepped aside and let Chip enter just as Gerri came back from her bathroom duty.

Chip looked up at the stranger.

"This is my sister, Gerri," Maggie said. "Gerri, this is Chip McGill."

"Pleased to meet you," he said, extending his hand. He was used to people hesitating before shaking, as if he might be dirty, but Gerri smiled and took his hand warmly.

She's sizing him up, Maggie thought. *The local handyman with a drinking problem. Which one of them should I warn?*

"Chip's here to work on the fireplace. *I'm* having it redone." She was pleased with herself for not saying "we" this time. "He's a chimney sweep, too."

"That I am," said Chip. "I'll get my tools."

He headed back out to his beat-up blue truck, parked on the street in front of the house.

"Time to get started on the rest of my day," Maggie said, leaving the door open for Chip. "I have to go to the factory. You're welcome to come."

"No," replied Gerri. "I think today is a good time for me to explore this town. I never really saw much on my last visit. It's home now. We should get to know each other."

The words were not comforting to Maggie. She wasn't sure she wanted her sister living with her for more than a few weeks.

"You do that," said Maggie. "If you need any suggestions ..."

"I like to explore, don't worry. I'll be fine."

Gerri headed upstairs to get ready for a day of sightseeing while Maggie waited for Chip to return with his toolbox.

The fireplace in the Dahl's house was original, dating back to the house's construction sometime in the early 1920s. The brick had once been red but had turned black with soot around the opening. Then, at some point, occupants of the house decided not to use it at all and had painted it brown—a hideous brown, in Maggie's opinion. She only knew about the soot after Chip had started stripping the paint. He said it was the only way to get it back to its original feel and look. Once the paint was completely stripped off he would set about restoring it as best he could, and replacing any damaged bricks.

Chip had started helping David with the house two weeks after they'd moved in. They'd been referred to him by their neighbors, who had used him to fix up their kitchen.

"He drinks a lot," Alice had told them disapprovingly, in the only negative reaction they'd had to hiring Chip. Maggie wondered at the time if Chip and Alice had a history, but she wrote it off as Alice being judgmental.

Maggie knew very little about Chip or his story, except that he had been in Lambertville his entire life.

He'd had a wife at one point but something had caused them to part—he didn't talk about it—and he had a daughter, Heather, who ran an art gallery in town. He lived above Davies' Hardware, which Maggie knew because she had gone there once to pay him. (He'd called the house sounding in no condition to drive, asking if they could please pay him in cash this time, so Maggie had walked over to his apartment and given him $100 for the previous day's work.) Contrary to Alice's impression of Chip, they had both liked him and trusted him, to the point David had given him a key to the house so he could come and go as he needed to work on the renovation.

Gerri had left for her neighborhood exploration twenty minutes earlier. Maggie was watching Chip strip paint off the bricks, hoping the smell of the solvent would not make them sick. Checks was curled on a chair, disinterested.

Chip had acknowledged the cat without commenting on him. She knew he was a very private man who extended that sense of privacy to everyone else: if Maggie wanted him to know anything about Checks, she would tell him. Otherwise it was none of his business.

"Say, Chip," Maggie said, after thinking for several minutes about how to approach this particular subject.

"Yeah, Mrs. Dahl ..." he said, less a question than a statement. He didn't seem to be paying her much attention.

"I was wondering ... if somebody needed to borrow some money ..."

He stopped what he was doing but did not turn around. He'd been hunched down with his back to her.

"Yeah?"

89

"Well, if someone needed, say, cash in a hurry ..."

He swiveled on his haunches and looked up at her. "Are you having troubles, Mrs. Dahl? With the business?"

Horrified, Maggie quickly said, "Oh no, I'm not talking about me."

He peered at her. "Who, then?"

Here we go, thought Maggie. *I hate lying.* But she did it anyway.

"I have a friend ... I can't say who, he would be so embarrassed."

She glanced toward the stairs, deliberately hinting that her friend was in fact her sister.

"But he can't get a loan at the bank, and it's not even that much money. Just a few thousand dollars. I'm not in a position to help her ... him ... with the store opening and all. And you know pretty much everyone in town. I was just wondering if there was anyone who made ... off the books loans, that sort of thing."

"A loan shark, you mean."

"Is that what they call them?" She knew very well that's what they were called.

His expression darkened. "Why would you think I might know such a thing?"

"I ... I didn't, not necessarily, I just thought ..."

"Old Chip, he's got that criminal feel to him, kind of a derelict."

"Chip, please, that's not what I meant at all. I just thought, with all your connections ..."

"I'm connected well enough to pay my rent and that's about it, Mrs. Dahl. And I do appreciate the work you give me—everyone gives me—but that doesn't mean I'm familiar with the shady side of things."

"You know, Chip, you're right, forget I said

anything, please. I apologize."

He turned back away from her and started stripping the bricks again. Maggie was about to leave the room when he spoke.

"I've got a number you can call, but that's all I've got."

"A number?"

"A telephone number. Get a pencil and write it down. What you do with it and who you meet on the other end is not my business."

Maggie hurried to the coffee table and took a small writing pad and pencil from its bottom shelf.

With his back still to her, Chip said, "I've never called this number, as far as anyone is concerned. You understand?"

"Completely," Maggie said.

"And I sure hope your friend doesn't regret it. Please don't say where you got it."

"Not a word."

Chip proceeded to recite a phone number while Maggie wrote it down. She had no idea if this was the person Alice owed money to, or if it was in any way connected to her murder, but it was more to go on than she'd had before Chip arrived, which had been nothing at all.

CHAPTER Fourteen

MAGGIE DROVE TO THE FACTORY after her talk with Chip, the phone number he'd given her safely tucked into a sleeve of her wallet. It was a Pennsylvania number—she knew that from the area code—and she wondered if it was someone in Philadelphia. That would make sense, given its proximity to Lambertville. You could get to Philly in an hour.

Gerri was somewhere in town, probably having cappuccino and a scone at one of the popular coffee places on Bridge Street. Maggie remembered how much pleasure she and David had taken in sitting by a window watching the locals and tourists walk by on a Saturday morning. They were at a table at one of the coffee shops when David first said he could see them living there.

Wherever Gerri was, she had not felt a need to call or text her sister. This was a good sign: maybe Gerri's presence in her home was something Maggie could adjust to after all. As long as they had their own lives and devoted themselves to separate activities, it might work out. She knew Gerri wanted to help with Dahl House Jams. She wasn't sure she could take being around her sister as much as that would entail, but she needed help running the store once it opened. She would have to give it careful thought.

She'd expected to see everyone at the factory— Gloria, Sybil, Peter and Janice. Their big shipment had gone out, giving them a little room to breathe, relax and celebrate. Assuming all went well with the order for Hearth and Home, they could find themselves busier than ever within weeks. Maggie tried not to think of the alternative—that their jams could flop in a chain store that size. They had all told themselves failure was not an option. They'd already found their jams and jellies in local restaurants and people were talking: *When will the store open? How can I get some for my grandparents? Can we order them online?* Maggie made a note to herself to check with Cathy Ashby, the young web wizard who had designed their site. It was up and running but Maggie had requested some changes and she hadn't had time to see if they'd been done.

She parked in her front spot and headed into the factory. They had several smaller orders to get out, plus what she needed to stock the store for the opening. She walked inside, suddenly aware she hadn't thought about Alice Drapier or her tragic death for the past twenty minutes. She was thinking how quickly it had consumed her attention when she saw Sybil and Gloria in the front office, whispering.

"Morning, ladies," Maggie said. "Where's Janice?"

They stopped talking, turning worried gazes to Maggie.

"Is something wrong?" asked Maggie. "Is Janice okay?"

"She's fine, Mrs. Dahl," said Gloria. The younger of the two cousins, she was a slim 40-something with a long reddish ponytail that draped to the middle of her back. Maggie knew she had two sons and a husband, Jim, who worked for the post office. She had been the Dahls' first hire, and she had recommended both Sybil, her maternal cousin, and Peter Stapley. "She's running late, she called."

Janice was as reliable as anyone Maggie knew so she wasn't alarmed by that, but something was troubling the women.

"It's Peter," Sybil said, glancing nervously at the door that led into the factory proper.

Maggie slipped her purse into a bottom file drawer. "Is he sick? Did something happen?"

Sybil was in her fifties. Her daughter had left home some years ago and now lived in Arizona with twin sons Sybil often bragged about. She'd been a widow much longer than Maggie, and working at the factory had given a new chapter to her life.

"Something happened," said Gloria, her voice low, "ten years ago today."

"Oh my gosh," Maggie said, knowing immediately what they were talking about. Peter's daughter Lilly had vanished, never to be found, and apparently today was the ten year anniversary. "Poor Peter. Has he said anything about it?"

"He never talks about it, Mrs. Dahl," Gloria said.

"He can't," added Sybil.

While the whole town knew the story of Lilly Stapley disappearing at the age of twelve, it was not something Peter ever discussed. His life had been shattered by it. His wife had left him, and for a number of years he had been unable to work—unable to *function* — beyond a bare minimum that kept him alive. Maggie knew from what the cousins had told her that Peter had sold his house and his belongings, whatever would provide enough money to keep a roof over his head. He'd worked subsistence-level jobs since then, living in a converted garage, and Maggie had been grateful she could offer him a decent wage and a place to go every day.

"Let me say good morning to him," Maggie said. The women started to protest, but said nothing. They knew Maggie would not pressure Peter. She would be gentle with him, and if he didn't want to talk—which they knew he wouldn't—she would leave it alone.

Maggie walked past them, back into the factory. David had installed a wall between front and back to provide privacy in the main office. It also helped keep out the sounds of jam making on a modest scale.

Peter was at one of the vats, checking the gauges. He jumped when Maggie came up beside him.

"Morning," he said, his back to her.

"Good morning, Peter," she said. "How's it going?"

He remained turned away from her. "Fine, we're doing the mixberry for the store opening."

Mixberry was one of their signature and most popular flavors. David had come up with it. Remembering it made Maggie wince

"Excellent." Using the vat as an excuse, Maggie walked up to it and peered in. It positioned her in front of Peter. "David loved that smell," she said, turning to face him.

She was shocked by what she saw. His eyes were bloodshot from crying and his face was drawn. He quickly looked down at the floor.

"I'm sorry, Peter," she said. "I know today is an anniversary ..."

"We need another word," he said. "'Anniversary' is a celebration, something you're happy about."

He was right. *Anniversary* was the wrong word when it came to something so horrific as the abduction of a child.

"I won't press you, Peter, but if you ever want to talk about it ..."

"Don't wait for that," he said. "It won't happen."

Maggie stood there a moment, letting his sorrow hang in the air. There was nothing she or anyone else could do about it. It was *his* grief, his despair. She knew something about that, having dealt the last six months with friends wanting her to *talk about her feelings*. She knew the implicit message was that she should move on, that grief makes people uncomfortable and there was some timeline beyond which it felt like an imposition on others. She had not done as they'd hoped, but she had stopped talking about it to most people. She guarded her grief, just as Peter Stapley guarded his.

She was relieved to hear Janice coming in the front door. It provided her a graceful exit from an awkward situation.

"I'll leave you to it," she said, "but you know I'm here." She gently put her hand on Peter's arm.

"I know that, thank you."

She nodded and left him alone.

The rest of the morning was surprisingly uneventful, given how much Maggie needed to get done and how little time there was to do it. She'd been consumed by the order for Hearth and Home for the past three weeks, from the time it first came in and sent them all into a state of delirium, to the moment it got shipped out and they were able to breathe—and pray. It was as close to a make-or-break order as they would ever have, given how precarious the birth of a business can be.

If you make it a year you can make it ten, Maggie thought. It was hard to go on without David, but one thing she did not allow herself in his absence was the possibility of not succeeding. Thinking that Dahl House Jams & Specialties might not be around in a year caused her to chasten herself—*stop that, right now ... David is listening.* It wasn't the first time she'd imagined such a thing; losing someone so much a part of yourself does strange things to you after the damage has been done. It leaves you with ghost limbs, phantom caresses, and fanciful ideas like being listened to by the departed.

She shook it off and told Janice she needed to go to her car, she'd forgotten something in the glove compartment. Janice had been sitting at the front desk going over invoices. Maggie had not forgotten anything, she just wanted to make a very private phone call.

She left the factory and got into her car, leaning over and pretending to rummage through the glove compartment while she used her cell phone to dial the number Chip had given her. It rang several times and she was sure it would go into voicemail, when someone picked up.

"What?" said a man's voice.

That's how you answer the phone? Maggie thought. *'What'?*

"Hello?" the man said. "What's this call about?"

Sitting up now, visible to Janice through the front window, Maggie waved and smiled, as if she'd just happened to take a call from someone while she was in the car. Janice waved back.

"I was wondering ..." Maggie said, faltering.

"Where'd you get this number?"

"From a mutual friend," Maggie lied.

"We don't have mutual friends," said the man. "You've got five seconds to stop lying and tell me why you called this number."

"I need a loan!" Maggie blurted.

There was silence on the other end. "I'll ask you one more time, lady, where did you get this number?"

Maggie sighed. She could not keep lying to this man and expect him not to hang up on here. "Chip," she said, convinced he could hear her guilt over the phone. "Chip McGill. But he was only taking pity on me, please leave him out of it. I don't want to get him in any trouble."

"You think I'm trouble?"

Maggie could swear the man was amused. It annoyed her.

"No, Sir," she said. "I don't think anything at the moment. I was just hoping you could help me."

"It's possible. What did this Chip McGill say?"

"Pardon?"

"Did he tell you who you were calling?"

"No," said Maggie. "He just gave me the phone number, and I had to push him for that. He wasn't going to. This is entirely my idea."

More silence. "What kind of idea is that?"

"To borrow money. I'm opening a store, you see …"

"Do you have a name?"

"Maggie Dahl."

"Doll? Like the kid's toy?"

"No, D-A-H-L."

"Like the jams," he said.

Maggie was surprised. "So you've heard about us."

"They have your stuff at the breakfast place I go to."

He sounded less guarded now and Maggie hoped it meant he would meet her.

"Listen, lady, we don't discuss these things on the phone."

We? Was there more than one? Maggie wondered.

Or was it 'we' as in some kind of crime syndicate?

"I'm happy to meet you somewhere," she said.

"I'll think about it and call you back if the answer is yes."

"Don't you want my number?"

"It's called 'caller ID'" the man said, as if Maggie were a not-too-bright child. "I can see it right here on my phone. You're in Jersey."

"Oh, of course. Well listen, about the money, I'm a little short on time ..."

"Not my problem, Maggie."

After all the times she'd told people to call her Maggie instead of Mrs. Dahl, the way he said it sent a chill through her.

"Right. I appreciate your talking to me ..."

Click. The phone went dead. Whoever the man was, he'd decided the conversation was over.

She looked up and saw Janice watching her through the window. It wasn't an intrusive stare, not *prying*, but enough to remind Maggie she was sitting in her car having just called a loan shark.

She waved at Janice again, slid her phone into her sweater pocket and headed back inside.

CHAPTER Fifteen

"A *LOAN SHARK*?" GERRI SAID, astonished. "Are you out of your mind?"

They were eating a late lunch at Bernadette's, a popular restaurant on Union Street near Bridge, not too far from the Dahl House storefront. It had been a favorite of Maggie's and David's since they'd moved to Lambertville. The owner, a young woman named Rachel who had named the restaurant after her late mother, had taken a liking to the Dahls and knew what they each enjoyed for lunch. She still waited tables and had taken Gerri's order without even asking Maggie what she wanted—she already knew.

Their salads had arrived shortly afterward and they were halfway through them when Maggie explained her plan. She wanted to meet this mysterious loan shark and see if he could shed any light on the darker side of Alice Drapier's life.

The man had called Maggie back while she was on the other line with Gerri arranging to have lunch. She'd quickly finished the call with her sister, then gotten instructions from the man on when and where to meet him: the Java Flow in New Hope, 6:00 p.m. that evening.

"What do you look like?" she'd said to him. "How will I know you?"

"Don't worry about that," he'd replied. "I'll know you."

How he would recognize her was a mystery she did

not want to ponder too deeply. She'd agreed to be there at the arranged time and hung up, all the while glancing at the office door to make sure Janice and the others couldn't hear her. Then she'd hurried off to Bernadette's to meet Gerri for lunch.

"You could have come to me," Gerri said, spearing a piece of asparagus in her salad bowl. "I don't have much money, but still ..."

"You're not listening. I don't need money. This is not about borrowing cash from a loan shark. This is about trying to get information on what—and who—happened to Alice."

"And you believe he's just going to tell you what he knows, if he knows anything. Think about it, Maggie. If this man has information about Alice's death, wouldn't telling you be the last thing he would do? What if he's involved in it?"

"I have to try."

Gerri set her fork down. "And why is that? Why are you so invested in pursuing something that could have serious and possibly life-threatening consequences for you?"

"What consequences?"

"Let's start with getting yourself killed. Murderers don't like being apprehended. Have you thought about that?"

"I'm not going to chase him out of the coffee shop! And if he had something to do with her murder, don't you think he would have ignored me? I'll take whatever I find out straight to Sergeant Hoyt and let him deal with it. As for why I'm invested, I can't explain it. Guilt, I suppose."

"How ridiculous. Why would you feel guilty?"

Maggie finished her salad and slid the plate to the

side. "I keep thinking there's some connection between Alice coming into my house that morning and ending up dead in her kitchen."

"I don't see it. You're mistaking coincidence for fate."

"You're right, Gerri, I'm aware of that. There is no logical explanation for why I'm pursuing this. But I found her body, you understand? I rushed her out of my home, treating her like a nuisance, and I found her dead twelve hours later. I just feel a sense of responsibility."

"To Alice."

"To Alice ... and to the cat."

"Okay," Gerri said. "I know I can't stop you, but I can go with you."

"If he sees me there with someone else he may not show himself. Remember, I don't know what he looks like. He can just keep walking, or finish his coffee and leave, with me none the wiser."

"He won't know who I am. I'll find a parking spot in front, or nearby, and I'll just be there, inconspicuous, watching."

"I'm not sure that's a good idea."

"If I were you I wouldn't talk about good ideas, since this is all a bad one. But you're going to go because that's who you are, and I'm going with you. End of discussion."

She was right, Maggie knew. Gerri couldn't stop her from meeting the loan shark, and she couldn't stop Gerri from tagging along in the shadows. She waved at Rachel for the check. She needed to do some more work at the storefront. Gerri could help her, then they could drive over the bridge to New Hope and put their flimsiest of plans into action.

CHAPTER Sixteen

MAGGIE WANTED TO INSPECT EVERYTHING again, fretting over each shelf and its contents, the color scheme, the choices she had made for what to display and where to display it. David was supposed to help with all that, and Maggie felt his absence every time she walked through the door. They had looked at three empty stores before settling on one. She'd second guessed herself many times since then: was it the right location? Was it really affordable in the long run? Did she have what it takes to sustain the factory *and* succeed with a flagship store?

A flagship store ... She smiled at the thought. They had talked about making it a chain. For all his claims to want out of the big city, David had been a very ambitious man. Achieving was part of his nature, his DNA. He could no more *not* compete than he could stop breathing.

Poor choice of words, she thought. *He did stop breathing, and you didn't hear him. How long had he been dead when you tried to wake him, Maggie? How many hours had passed between his last breath and the terrifying realization you would never be able to say goodbye?*

"What's on your mind?" Gerri asked, startling Maggie out of her reverie.

They were moving customized jam jars from one shelf to another, more prominent, display case.

"Just thinking about it all. And how much I appreciate you being here."

"'Being here,'" Gerri said. "I notice you didn't say 'moving here.'"

"You've only been living with me for two days, let's give it some time."

Maggie knew her sister was worried it wouldn't work out and she would be forced into moving back to Philly, or, if that wasn't an option for Gerri, then somewhere else not too far away. The more she was honest with herself about the challenges she faced — from the factory and store to the house renovation, and from being half of a couple all her adult life to being alone — the more Maggie hoped it would work out with Gerri, at least for a while. A year, maybe two.

The women looked up at the sound of the bell. Maggie glanced at the door, sure she had left the 'Closed' sign facing out. She had.

A tall man wearing a blue and yellow windbreaker, tan Timberland boots, and a baseball cap with the words *Davies Hardware* stenciled across the front, stepped into the store and closed the door behind him.

"Afternoon, ladies," he said.

"Cal, how are you?" Maggie said. She knew Cal Davies from several trips she'd taken with David to the town's longest running hardware store. She didn't know much about the store's history, but she knew Davies had taken over from his father and that Davies Hardware had been established "circa 1959," according to a sign over the front window. Maggie guessed him to be in his mid-fifties.

"I'm doing well, Mrs. Dahl."

"We're not quite open yet."

"I can see that," he said, turning back and pointing at the sign. "I just thought you might need some help. I know Chip's been giving you a hand at the house."

At some point in time the elder Davies had purchased the building, kept his store in the ground floor retail space and rented out the three floors of apartments above it. Maggie had no idea if the Davies family had ever lived there, but she knew Cal Davies had a house on Delevan Street, two blocks over from her own.

"And doing a great job of it," Maggie said, a little too eagerly, as if she needed to vouch for Chip's work ethic. The truth was he'd been late a couple times and had once not shown up at all, rumored to have gone on a bender.

"Good to hear that," Cal said. "I've been a little worried about him."

"Really? Why would that be?"

"I don't know, he just seems more distracted than usual, like he's got something on his mind."

Maggie did not want to pursue the subject. She worried the more they said, the more likely they would be to discuss Chip's drinking problem when he wasn't there to defend himself.

Davies walked further into the room and looked around, nodding approvingly.

"You've done a great job here, ladies ..."

On the word *ladies* he tilted his head slightly and smiled at Gerri.

"This is my sister, Gerri Lerner," Maggie said, introducing them.

Gerri stepped up to Davies and extended her hand. "Pleased to meet you."

"Lerner ... Lerner ..." said Cal, as if trying to recall something about the name.

"That's my maiden name," Gerri said. "I'm not the sort who keeps an ex-husband's name. What's the point?"

Maggie could see Gerri making a quick estimation of the man. She knew Cal was a widower of some years and that he had no children. She remembered David telling her that after he'd first met Davies.

"I hope you like your visit," Cal said to Gerri, letting her hand go with a slight, additional brush of the fingertips.

"Oh, I'm more than visiting, Mr ...?"

"Davies," Maggie said quickly. "I'm so sorry. This is Cal Davies. He owns Davies Hardware. A lot of the work that Chip's been doing is with supplies from Cal's store."

"That's right." Cal looked down, averting his gaze. "I'm so sorry about Mr. Dahl. I wish we'd had more time to get to know each other."

"Thank you," said Maggie. "Now, I really should be getting back to work."

"What's the hurry?" Gerri said.

Maggie glared at her. "We have an appointment, and we should go home first, feed the cat, that sort of thing."

"You have a cat?" asked Cal. "Mr. Dahl never mentioned it. Not that he would! But we do sell litter, 'America's Finest Cat Litter,' to be exact. It says so on the package. I don't have a cat myself but I'm told it's good stuff."

"And I'm grateful for the suggestion. I've never had a cat before."

"I see," said Cal. "Is it something you decided after Mr. Dahl passed? To keep you company? I was tempted after my wife died but never went through with it."

"No, it wasn't because of that. Actually, Checks— the cat—belonged to my neighbor, Alice Drapier."

Cal looked at her. "What a terrible situation, and in a place like Lambertville."

"Awful," said Maggie. She did not want to get into a discussion about the murder, or the cat, or anything else. "I appreciate the information about the litter, truly. We'll stop by the store soon and you can remind me."

"Be sure to bring your sister," he said, turning and offering Gerri a small wave.

"I'll do that. And thank you again. I hope to see you at the opening."

Stepping outside, Cal said, "Absolutely. It's the biggest event we've got going, except for Halloween."

Maggie was reminded how quickly time passed. The store had to open before Halloween, and that was just around the corner.

"Thank you again for stopping by," she said, standing in the doorway while Cal walked up the street.

"What do you know about him?" Gerri asked.

"Wife died maybe fifteen years ago. No kids. A fixture in town. Nice guy. I have no information on his assets or his interest in women who've been divorced three times. Now grab your purse, we need to go home, then head to New Hope. I'd like to get there early. It's always better to see the other person coming."

"But you don't know what he looks like."

"And he doesn't know what I look like."

"You hope," Gerri said, letting the implication hang there. She picked up her purse from under the front counter and followed Maggie out of the store.

CHAPTER Seventeen

LOCATED ALONG THE DELAWARE RIVER in Buck's County, Pennsylvania, New Hope has been famous for decades as a tourist destination offering visitors a small but vibrant selection of shops, restaurants, bookstores, and the Buck's County Playhouse. Every now and then you could catch Broadway regulars performing shows when they weren't wowing audiences in Manhattan. A popular walking trail snakes alongside the river, and any summer day, rain or shine, the town's population swells several times its normal size with people driving in to enjoy its pleasures.

New Hope was where David had originally imagined moving to. Maggie was not as taken with the town and suggested they keep their options open rather than dive into something they might regret in six months. Then they'd walked across the bridge to New Jersey and found themselves in Lambertville. It was love at first sight.

"What's not to like about New Hope?" Gerri asked. She was driving, since Maggie planned to get out a block from the coffee shop while Gerri circled back for a parking spot.

"There's nothing not to like about it, I just prefer Lambertville. For one thing, there's no free parking in New Hope."

"It's a tourist town."

"But still, they have meters all the way to the town limit. It's not very inviting. Anyway, it doesn't matter.

We moved to Lambertville, I love it there, and I'm happy to visit New Hope. I can almost see it from my kitchen window."

It was an exaggeration but not by much: New Hope and Lambertville were effectively sister cities, and if you preferred one over the other, as Maggie did, all you had to do was walk or drive across the bridge to visit the other.

"There," Maggie said, pointing to a car pulling out from the curb.

"But I'm just dropping you off. I'll find something closer to the coffee shop."

"No, you won't. Take this spot while you can."

"Fine then," Gerri said, putting on her blinker and backing up as she parallel parked. "This will do. Just let me get ahead of you and find a seat."

"You're coming in?"

"Think about it, Maggie. What's more obvious? Me standing outside in the dark pretending not to watch through the window, checking my watch as if I'm meeting someone, or me sipping a cappuccino at a table on a cold October night?"

Maggie had to admit the sense of it. It would be better to have Gerri go inside first and situate herself where she could see what was happening.

"I'll act like I'm texting someone on my phone," Gerri said. "Everybody does it. I can laugh a little, act surprised."

"You mean you can draw attention to yourself."

"That's not what I meant," said Gerri. She turned the car off and grabbed her purse, slipping the keys inside.

"Give me five minutes," she said. "I'll be sitting down by the time you get there."

Maggie looked at her watch. She was ten minutes early. For all she knew, the man was already there, doing exactly what Gerri planned to do: sitting and watching who comes in the door. For that matter, he might think Gerri was her and make some kind of move.

"I'm not sure about this …"

"We can never really be sure about anything," Gerri said, sliding out of the car. "Remember, wait five minutes and under no circumstances are we to make eye contact."

Gerri slammed her door and headed up the street.

Remembering the meter, Maggie quickly took out a credit card and paid for an hour.

Nestled between an ice cream store that was closed half the year and a Mexican restaurant, the Java Flow was located on a prime stretch of Main Street, New Hope's central thoroughfare. Unlike many stores that had tried to make a go of it in the small but famous town, the Java Flow had survived for six years and showed every sign of continuing. Maggie didn't know the coffee shop well, although she and David had been there twice on their occasional walks across the river from Lambertville.

The interior was well lighted, which suited her purpose this evening. She'd done as Gerri asked and waited several minutes, then walked casually to the coffee shop. She could see three or four people at the half dozen tables inside, one of them being her sister who kept her head down, pretending to read the *Bucks County Herald*.

There was a man alone at one table. He looked up at Maggie when she walked in. Was he the loan shark?

How would she know? He didn't nod at her or acknowledge her in any way; he just looked up at the sound of the door opening, then went back to a book he was reading.

There were two people working behind the counter, one middle-aged woman who looked to be cleaning up at the end of the day, and a pimply-faced teenaged boy with braces and a ponytail.

"Can I help you?" the boy said when Maggie walked to the register. She glanced at the display case that held a couple leftover muffins and two slices of banana nut bread.

"I'll take a blueberry muffin," Maggie said, "and a decaf cappuccino."

The boy nodded and set about making the coffee.

Maggie took the opportunity for another look around. She was now certain she'd gotten there before the loan shark. She felt silly, wondering again how she would recognize the man and if he would be obvious — would he have some kind of TV-movie mob look to him? Would he come in wearing an ill-fitting brown suit and holding an unlit cigar?

She stole another glance at Gerri, who was doing a very good job of ignoring her. If Maggie didn't know better, she would think Gerri hadn't seen her come in. The man continued to read his novel. There was a young couple holding hands and talking excitedly at one table, and an older woman at another who was dressed in a woolen overcoat, with glasses on a gold necklace, blowing steam across the top of a tea cup. She smiled at Maggie.

Maggie smiled back.

They locked eyes a moment, then two, then three ... and it hit Maggie: *It's the old woman.*

"Excuse me?" the boy said behind her. Maggie did not hear him. She stared at the woman who'd met her gaze, then added a smile.

Maggie pointed at her, as if to say, "You?"

The woman nodded, smiled again and motioned to the chair across from her.

"Excuse me?" the boy repeated, this time slightly irritated.

"Oh, yes, I'm sorry," Maggie said, turning back around. She quickly paid for the muffin and cappuccino, then took them to the table where the woman was waiting.

"May I sit here?" Maggie asked.

"Please do, Mrs. Dahl." She added bluntly, "Who's the other woman? Is that your sister?"

Maggie blushed, feeling her face go hot. "How did you …"

"I make it my business to know who I'm dealing with," the woman said. "Let's just say we have a mutual source."

Chip, thought Maggie. Of course he would tell this woman he'd given Maggie the number to call.

"My name's Dahlia, by the way," the woman said, offering her hand as Maggie sat down. "Dahlia Getty."

Maggie looked at her curiously.

"What, you were expecting someone Italian? This isn't the movies."

"I was expecting someone *male*," Maggie said. "The man I spoke to on the phone."

"He works for me. Quite a few people do. Someone in my position has to be careful. Now, enjoy your muffin, then we'll talk … in very broad terms, you never know who's listening anymore."

"Oh," said Maggie, surprised. "I'm not *wired*, if

that's what you mean."

"I don't mean anything, Mrs. Dahl. Now please, you paid for your treat, have a few bites and we'll talk."

Maggie nodded. She wanted to glance at Gerri but knew there was no point in it. Dahlia Getty, if that was her name, already knew who Gerri was. Maggie had the sinking feeling she'd been had. Now she just wanted to get whatever information she could from this woman and go home. She was feeling unsafe and unprepared, exposed in the light of the coffee shop. She looked out the window as she took a bite of her muffin, wondering if someone was out there watching them. The man who'd told her to come here? Someone else who worked for Dahlia Getty? She suddenly felt as if she could not trust reality itself, it had shifted and swirled and taken her by surprise so completely the last few days.

She washed a bite of muffin down with a sip from her cappuccino, then wiped her fingers on a napkin and looked directly at the woman across from her. It was time to talk.

"I know quite a bit about you already," Dahlia Getty said. Whatever herbal tea she had was cool enough now for her to take a sip. She let some rest in her mouth, then swallowed and placed the cup back on its saucer.

"And how do you know all this?" Maggie asked.

"I'm a businesswoman. And a smart one."

"You're a loan shark."

Getty smiled at her. "I help people in difficult situations. What concerns me is that given what I've learned about you, you just don't seem like someone who would use my services."

"And you," Maggie said, returning the smile, "don't seem like someone who offers them."

The woman laughed, and Maggie got the impression it was sincere. There was something admittedly absurd about the whole thing. They were in a coffee shop in an upscale artists' haven known for a few restaurants and a playhouse. They were sitting at a table near a window, looking for all the world like two old friends getting caught up after a day of shopping. The setting itself was ridiculous, and to be meeting about something as shady as a cash loan made outside the law was laughable.

They had not kept their voices down, but no one in the shop appeared to hear them or want to — except Gerri, who Maggie imagined was frustrated by the turn of events. Whatever her sister had expected, this was not it.

"I took over for my father," Getty said. "If that helps support your stereotypes, although he didn't look any more like a ... loan officer ... than I do.

"Now let's get to the truth of it, Mrs. Dahl. You're not here to borrow money, are you?"

"No, I'm not. And if I had to I would go to a bank, I can assure you that."

"No need to."

"I'm here because my neighbor was murdered."

"Alice Drapier."

Maggie started to ask how she knew, then realized it was pointless. Dahlia Getty would have known two days ago that Alice was dead. Possibly even before the rest of the town, given the sort of underworld network she must be part of.

"I understand you found her," Getty said.

Maggie stared at her. Was there anything she didn't

know? And if that was the case, what sort of game were they playing?

"I did," said Maggie. "And I found her cat, and I found her debt, and I found you. So ... since you know everything, I'm hoping you can tell me who would want her dead."

"Certainly not me."

"But she owed you money."

Getty sipped her tea again. "First, I would have no reason to kill someone who owed me money, even if that was something I had an interest in doing. Remember, Mrs. Dahl, I'm a financier, not a murderer. It's not a very good business plan to end the lives of people before they pay you back, and once they have there's no reason to. Secondly, she didn't owe me any money."

Maggie was surprised. "But I thought ..."

"You didn't think. You made assumptions, the first one being that Alice Drapier borrowed money from me."

She was right, Maggie thought. Chip had simply connected her with the man on the phone. He had said nothing about Alice borrowing money, let alone from the woman she was speaking to.

"You're clever, I'll give you that," Dahlia continued. "But you were only half right. Heather McGill settled Mrs. Drapier's account. I'm not owed anything, and had I not been intrigued by you we wouldn't be sitting here."

Maggie watched her, confused.

"Don't you want the rest of your muffin?"

"No, I'm not hungry. I just ... why would Chip's daughter buy Alice's debt?"

"You'd have to ask her that," Dahlia said. "And I'm

sure you will. Now if you'll excuse me, I'm feeling overexposed here."

Getty stood up, taking a five dollar bill from her wallet and leaving it on the table.

"If you knew I didn't want to borrow money from you, why risk coming here?" Maggie asked. "It couldn't be just to meet me."

Getty glanced around the coffee shop. "I liked Alice. She didn't deserve to die like that. But I'm not a *sleuth*, I don't go chasing killers ... or loan sharks. Partly because they might chase you back. Take that as a warning, Mrs. Dahl. Now I really must go."

The Getty woman said nothing more, walking to the door. She gave a quick wave to the woman behind the counter, who nodded back at her. As soon as she left, the young couple and the old man who'd been the only other people in the shop got up and left also, leaving just Maggie, the baristas, and a dumbfounded Gerri.

Did they all work for her? Maggie wondered, stunned. Maybe the shop itself was a front of some kind.

She had just met one of the strangest people she'd ever encountered, possibly one of the most dangerous, yet she was relieved. Whatever her motive, Dahlia Getty had done a good deed for poor, dead Alice. She had given Maggie a clue and left. What Maggie did with it was up to her.

"What just happened?" Gerri said. She was standing now, waiting for them to leave.

"I'm not sure," Maggie said. "But I won't soon forget it. Now let's go. I'm tired, I'm hungry, and I have to speak to someone tomorrow I've never met before."

"You ladies have a good night," the young counterman said, stepping around from behind the cash register to clear the tables.

Maggie thanked him and held the door for Gerri. She was ready to be gone from New Hope's version of the Twilight Zone.

CHAPTER Eighteen

WHAT STARTED OUT AS A strange evening ended plainly. Maggie and Gerri split a mushroom pizza while they watched reruns of Dateline and talked about everything except what had happened the past forty-eight hours. Gerri had pried at first, trying to get Maggie to tell her what she'd discussed with the odd woman at the coffee shop. All the way back in the car she'd peppered Maggie with questions: what was the woman's name? Was she really a loan shark? What did she say that had them leaving so abruptly?

Maggie told her the basics. The conversation with Dahlia Getty had not lasted long, so retelling it took barely more time than crossing the bridge back into New Jersey. She did not speculate about Heather McGill, mostly because she knew nothing about the woman, what sort of relationship she had with her father, or why she would pay off Alice's gambling debt. She wanted to let it all sit in her mind until morning. Then, when she'd woken up with a clear head and a good night's sleep, she would tell Gerri their next destination: an art gallery in Lambertville to talk to the daughter of a handyman who might just be the key to it all. Or not. She was prepared for any eventuality on a road that had already surprised her with its twists and turns.

By the time the 11:00 o'clock news came on, Maggie had had enough. She was usually in bed by 10:00 and had only stayed up later because she'd been excited and agitated about the trip to New Hope, and because her sister was an insomniac who'd wanted company.

They said good night, and Maggie left Gerri sitting on the couch watching news from Philadelphia while she went upstairs to bed. She hadn't seen Checks since they'd come home but wasn't concerned about it. He was clearly a cat of independent means and might have found a way out of the house, even though Maggie was sure there was none. She'd taken a liking to the animal. A house that had been empty, lonely and sometimes haunted without David, had become full and active the last few days. She paused on her way upstairs and looked around, wondering if David's spirit was amused. *So you thought you'd spend the rest of your life alone, Maggie? Think again.*

She situated herself in bed with her head propped on two pillows. She'd been reading a book of essays by a local writer named Shanna Delaney about life in small town New Jersey and the many insights it provided into the human condition. The book was a minor sensation and had made the author a local celebrity. Maggie had seen Delaney in town. She'd often noticed her sitting at the Beanery coffee shop on Bridge Street in the early mornings, with a laptop and cup of coffee at a small table in the corner as she worked on her book. Maggie sometimes went there for coffee and muffins for the office. Once the book came out, Delaney was more likely to be seen at the center of a small group of fans stroking the author's ego or offering their own pearls of wisdom gained from life along the river.

Maggie wasn't sure how deep the writer's insights were or how much of the book was manufactured hype, but she'd liked the half dozen pieces she'd read so far. Each one was just long enough to put her to sleep. She'd used the book instead of chamomile tea or, God forbid, a sleeping pill to help her drift off. By the time she got to the last sentence of a piece about local eating habits, her eyes were heavy and she'd slipped into that state where sleep had more sway than wakefulness. She glanced at the clock as she set the book on her nightstand and turned off the light: 11:45 p.m. Within two minutes she was asleep.

David was pouting again. He got that way when they argued. Conflict between them was rare and had amounted to little more than forceful opposition when one of them wanted one thing and the other wanted something else. The move to New Jersey had been an example: David had wanted to pack their belongings into a U-Haul and leave New York the day after they'd come back from their second trip to Lambertville. Maggie had been hesitant, stressing that they needed to think things through—*everything*—including the impact a move would have on their son, as well as what it meant for their financial future. The biggest bone of contention had been the apartment in Manhattan. Maggie wanted to rent it out, just in case they weren't as happy in Lambertville as they imagined they would be. David was firmly for selling. So they'd compromised and offered the apartment to Wynn. He'd declined, having no interest in living in the same apartment he'd grown up in. Maggie had finally agreed with David: it was highly unlikely they would return to the city, but if they did, they'd be ready to downsize anyway. And they needed the money. Dahl House Jams needed the money. The sale of the apartment was about financing their dreams, so they put it on the block and sold it within two months. Neither of them looked back—David because he was ready to move forward, and Maggie because she didn't want to deal with the emotions she'd find there.

He was sitting on the edge of the bed again, where he usually was in her dreams. His back was to her and she kept calling his name, "David … David, look at me when I'm talking to you." She reached out and put her hand on his naked shoulder. He'd slept nude all his life, and he'd been naked when he died. It had added to Maggie's horror when she'd shaken his corpse, trying to wake him from an eternal sleep.

"What did I say wrong this time?" she asked. "What did I do? I'm trying so hard, David. My sister's here now. And I have a cat. A cat! You didn't like cats. Is that it? You're upset that I have a cat?"

She heard meowing, as if mentioning cats to her dead husband had set one crying. The more she tried to pay attention to the sound in her dream, the more the dream began to tumble away from her. The meowing became yowling, and she swam as quickly as she could to the surface of consciousness. David vanished. The dream vanished. Maggie opened her eyes and gasped: Checks was pawing the pillow by her head, crying loudly and urgently.

"What is *wrong* with you, cat?"

She shoved Checks away from her and sat up in bed. She peered into the darkness of the bedroom. And then she heard it. Movement downstairs. She thought at first it must be Gerri, sleepless and raiding the kitchen for a midnight snack. She glanced at the clock: 2:45 a.m. Gerri's insomnia wasn't that bad. She would have gone to her bedroom an hour or two earlier. And then there was Checks, who'd lowered his meowing but persisted in pawing at the mattress. She heard it again—a creaking sound from downstairs. She thanked God it was an old house, the kind with floorboards and stairs that made lots of noise when you moved on them. She petted Checks, as much to silence him as to calm him. Then she quickly sat on the edge of the bed and reached for the nightstand drawer.

She'd kept David's gun. One of their pleasures as a couple was shooting—a pastime they did not discuss with most of their friends, unless those friends also had memberships to the Amsterdam Rifle and Pistol Range, located across town on Amsterdam Avenue just a few blocks from Lincoln Center. They'd enjoyed going for a night of theater, jazz or opera, followed by an hour of target practice. It wasn't something most of their friends would appreciate, so they'd kept that particular passion to themselves. After David died Maggie sold her gun, not because she suddenly didn't like guns, but because it was something they'd done together. The thought of firing a gun, or even holding one without David, had been too much for her. But for safety's sake, and because it had been *his*, she'd kept his Glock 17 9mm handgun. The first commercial model offered by Glock, it remained popular and David had chosen it the first time he'd seen it. That had been fifteen years ago. Now David was gone but the gun was still there. Maggie leaned down, took the grip and lifted it out of the drawer.

Unlike David, she did not sleep naked. Wearing her nightgown, she slid her feet onto the floor, held the Glock at her side, and carefully tiptoed to the bedroom door.

Checks stopped moving, as if he knew it was time to be quiet.

Maggie said a silent prayer to the god of hinges, turned the knob and opened her door. It squeaked only a little as she swung it open and stepped halfway into the hallway.

She could see Gerri's bedroom door. It was closed, and the light from a television cast moving shadows on the floor beneath it. Maggie knew Gerri slept with the TV on and the volume turned down.

She heard another sound — distinctly downstairs, and not her sister.

"I'm armed!" she called out. "If someone's in this house, leave now. I have a right to shoot you."

She waited and listened. Whoever was downstairs, if anyone was and it hadn't been the house settling or her imagination, stopped moving.

Maggie carefully walked into the hallway, making her way to the top of the stairs. She peered over the railing and saw nothing: the house was in darkness. She raised the gun in both hands and headed down.

She felt cold air. She could see the front door as she slowly descended one stair at a time. The door was closed: the air was not coming from there.

She considered calling out again but decided not to. If there was an intruder, it would announce her position and make her an easier target.

She nearly fell when Checks came barreling past her, jumping down the stairs ahead of her. She wondered if this crazed cat was trying to protect her. He sped around the main floor and into the kitchen.

Maggie took the last step down and stood still, listening. There were no more sounds, no more indications of movement. Still keeping the gun raised, she made her way into the kitchen and was hit by a blast of cold October air.

The back door stood open. She stared past it into the darkness of her backyard. She knew she'd locked it—she rarely used the back entrance and had been sure everything was locked since Alice had wandered into the house.

She let the gun ease to her side, then hurried to the back door and closed it. As she did, she looked at the lock, as well as the glass in the door and the door frame. There was no sign of forced entry. That meant whoever had come into her house had used a key.

She shut the door and locked it, checking the handle to be sure. She turned and saw Checks sitting on his haunches, staring up at her.

"Thanks," she said grudgingly.

"What's going on?"

Maggie nearly jumped out of her nightgown.

"Is that a gun in your hand?" Gerri asked. "Jesus, Maggie, when did you get a gun?"

Maggie and David's gun hobby was not something she'd told her sister about. She'd judged Gerri to be the anti-gun sort many years ago and had never felt like having an argument over it.

"It's David's," Maggie said, engaging the safety. The only person she might shoot at the moment was Gerri, and she didn't want to take any chances. "I had my own, by the way, and no, we're not going to discuss it."

"So answer my question: what's going on? It's three o'clock in the morning."

"It's nothing. I thought I heard someone."

"In the house? That's your idea of nothing?"

"Nothing I can be sure of," Maggie said, walking slowly past her out of the kitchen

"You're confusing me," said Gerri, following her into the hallway.

"I'm going to try and sleep now, we'll talk in the morning."

Moments later Maggie was back in bed, with Checks beside her. He faced away from her, staring at the door as if he'd decided to be a sentry for the rest of the night.

"You are one strange animal," Maggie said. "But I could love you. Just give me time."

She let her hand fall to the nightstand, making sure the drawer was open and the gun within reach.

DAY 4

"I believe cats to be spirits come to earth. A cat, I am sure, could walk on a cloud without coming through."

– Jules Verne

CHAPTER Nineteen

MAGGIE CONSIDERED HERSELF LUCKY TO have slept at all. She'd gone back to bed after what she was certain had been an intruder's entry into her home thinking sleep would be impossible, but she'd been wrong. Checks had done his part, settling onto the pillow beside her—David's pillow, covered with the same pillowcase that had been on it the night he died, and that she'd not washed since—and purring like a furry white noise machine. She was quickly becoming attached to the cat. Never a pet person, she'd been especially leery of felines. She'd met too many that confirmed people's suspicions about these particular animals: that they were calling the shots in any household they ran, and their human companions merely served at their pleasure. Checks, while displaying some of those tendencies, had also proven to be highly intelligent and, in the case of the suspected intruder, a possible life saver. *He didn't save Alice, did he?* Maggie thought as she got out of bed, Checks immediately hopping to the floor when she moved. *No, but I bet he would have if he could have.* She put on her robe and headed to the kitchen.

Gerri was already up, eating a piece of seven grain bread slathered with apricot jam, one of Dahl House Jams' first recipes. David had gotten it from his sister, who'd received it from their grandmother.

"What's up?" Gerri said, wiping her mouth with a napkin. She was sitting at the island counter they'd installed, part of the house renovations Maggie was now continuing alone. A smaller table was nestled against a wall, though Maggie seldom used it now that her husband no longer sat across from her.

"I slept, believe it or not," said Maggie, walking to the coffee pot and pouring herself a cup.

"I was talking to the cat."

Checks had padded into the kitchen on Maggie's heels. He'd taken up position between the women and was staring at Gerri, eyeing the toast.

"What's he doing?" continued Gerri. "Cat's don't eat toast."

Maggie ignored her. She spooned nondairy creamer into her coffee, and shoved a piece of bread into the toaster for herself.

"I think I should go to the police," said Maggie.

"About what?"

"About someone coming into my home in the middle of the night! What else would I be talking about?"

Gerri waited a moment, then said, "Maggie, you know I love you, so I can say this. Are you *sure* someone was in the house last night and that it wasn't a dream, or you weren't just hearing things? This is an *old* house, they make noises."

Maggie detected judgment in the way her sister called the house 'old.' She was tempted to tell Gerri no one was forcing her to stay there, but she bit her tongue and plated her toast instead. She took it to the counter, sat next to Gerri and put jam on her bread.

"The back door was open," Maggie said. "I felt the cold air when I was coming downstairs, and when I got into the kitchen the door was definitely open."

"Maybe you left it that way."

"Are you *gaslighting* me?"

Gerri looked at her, perplexed.

"It's from a movie," explained Maggie. "Never mind. Just know this: I heard someone moving around, I came downstairs—"

"With a gun," Gerri interrupted. "Remind me to talk to you about that."

"We'll never have that conversation. It's David's gun and I'm keeping it. There's nothing political in owning a firearm."

"It makes a statement, Maggie."

"Yes, it says, 'I have gun and if you don't get out of my house I will shoot you.' That's all the statement it needs to make. Now stop changing the subject."

"Fine. Someone was in the house. You left the backdoor unlocked, which I understand is a habit you have …"

"Not since Alice Drapier invited herself into my living room," Maggie said. "Doors are now locked, and I check to make *sure* they're locked. No, this was someone with …"

Gerri waited for her to finish. When she didn't, Gerri prompted her. "What, Maggie? What was this someone with?"

"A key."

Gerri ate the last bit of her toast, wiped her mouth off and said, "Please tell me you had the locks changed on this house."

Maggie looked away.

"Oh, for God's sake," said Gerri. "The first thing you do in a new home is change the locks."

"We meant to, but then we got busy with the business and the house renovations and everything else."

"Who has keys?"

"Pardon me?"

"I said, who has keys to our house?"

'Our house.' The words weren't lost on Maggie and she was not sure how she felt at the moment about her sister referring to the house as 'ours.'

"I don't know, really," Maggie said. "The realtor, the previous owners."

"And where are they?"

"Seattle. The wife's father has health problems so they moved there to take care of him. The house had been empty for two years. They let it fall into disrepair. That's what David liked about the place—he wanted something that needed work."

"Who else had keys?"

Maggie remained silent, thinking about it.

"*Everyone they ever gave keys to,*" Gerri said, answering her own question. "That's why you change them. You have no idea who has keys to your own house. I'm surprised at you, Maggie."

"Not as surprised as you were to see a Glock in my hand."

"What's a Glock?"

"Never mind," said Maggie. "While I'm thinking about who has keys to my house—my house, Gerri, let's wait a little while for the 'our' business—and getting the locks changed, we should have a conversation with Sergeant Hoyt again."

Gerri didn't respond to Maggie's comment about calling the house theirs. Instead she slid off the chair and said, "I can't this morning. I have a breakfast date."

"You just ate!"

"A single, lonely piece of toast with a drop of jam. It's not a proper breakfast. I'm doing small meals these days anyway, six or seven, with fruit for snacks. I've lost three pounds in two months. It's amazing."

Maggie ignored the dieting advice. "Who are you having breakfast with?"

"Tom Brightmore," Gerri said. "He owns—"

"The Brightside Diner," Maggie finished. "I know who he is. I also know he's quite a bit younger than you."

Gerri stared at her. "Is that ageism I hear, sister?"

"No. I just mean ..."

"I know what you mean. I know what everybody means with comments like that, and I don't care. If I was a man going out with a woman ten years my junior I'd be applauded."

"So you're going out with him now?"

"You're exasperating me, Maggie, please stop. No, we're not going out. I had coffee there the other day when I was exploring my new home—*my* new home, I can say that without your permission—and he was very friendly. We chatted. He told me about himself. I did the same."

"Did you leave out the part about three husbands?"

"It's best to reveal oneself a little at a time," said Gerri. "I will tell him when it's appropriate. For now, today, we're having breakfast, and *not* at his restaurant. That's gauche. We're going to the River Run Café."

"Nice," Maggie said, surprised. The River Run had amazing views of the Delaware River. "I hope he's paying."

"I'll pretend to offer," Gerri said, smiling. "He'll tell me he's got it. I'll drop my wallet back into my purse, and we'll see what comes of it all."

"Well, good luck, if that's the right thing to say. Just be careful. He's younger, you're starting a new life, take it all very easy. Meanwhile, I'll be going to the police station. Having an intruder come into my home at 3:00 a.m. is not something to ignore. At the very least I should file a report."

"I won't disagree with you. I'm just not sure what you're going to tell him, considering your habit of leaving the doors unlocked."

"Past habit."

Gerri started to leave the kitchen. She stopped at the doorway. "Are you planning to tell Sergeant Hoyt about your gun?"

"David's gun."

"*Whatever.* The one you had in your hand last night."

"I don't see any reason to," said Maggie. "It's licensed, and it's nobody's business. If it's going to gnaw at you, I'd suggest you forget about it."

"It's a hard sight to forget. Now if you'll excuse me, I have to get ready."

"Tell Tom Brightmore I said hello. They use our jams at his restaurant."

"I'll do no such thing," Gerri replied. She waved her fingers at Maggie and left the room.

Maggie proceeded to eat her toast, wondering about who had keys to her house. She'd make a list if she had any idea who to put on it. For now she needed to get ready. With less than a week until the store's opening, there was more work planned to prepare the interior. It had all been thoroughly cleaned, and now it was time to pay special attention to the details. Every little decoration, every stroke of paint, mattered.

She would stop and have a conversation with Sergeant Hoyt on her way to the store. If he advised her to file a police report, she'd do that, too. She couldn't shake the thought that the whole experience had been meant to frighten her. It had succeeded, of course, but who was behind it, and what they were trying to tell her, remained a mystery.

"Let's go," Maggie said to Checks. "Time's wasting."

She left her half-finished piece of toast on the plate. She grabbed her coffee cup and headed back upstairs, with Checks sauntering slowly after her. The more Maggie was around him, the more she knew he was born sure of himself. It was a trait she envied.

CHAPTER Twenty

MAGGIE COULDN'T TELL WHAT SERGEANT Hoyt thought of her. He was a difficult man to read. She wondered if his stoicism was part of his personality, or something he'd developed from his years on the police force. She assumed a certain detachment was necessary in a job that included dealing with criminals, community members and the occasional corpse. She thought these things as she sat across from him in the same conference room she'd been in with her sister during their previous visit to the station. He'd offered her coffee again and she'd accepted, happy to have a prop between them while she told him about the previous night's intruder.

"You actually heard someone downstairs?" he asked.

He'd hadn't acted all that surprised to see her. Maggie wondered if, after finding her and Gerri hiding in Alice Drapier's basement stairwell, he'd come to expect this kind of thing from her.

"I was dreaming ..." she started to say.

"Dreaming?"

He made another note on a yellow legal pad. He had not turned on the recorder this time. She wondered if he kept a file on her.

"Yes, but the sound wasn't part of the dream. The cat woke me up."

"So you heard meowing?"

She began to feel patronized. She looked at him to

see if there was any hint of a smile on his lips.

"*Urgent* meowing," she emphasized. "That's what woke me up. It's like Checks knew someone was in the house and he was trying to warn me."

"Checks is the cat?"

"Yes, at least he inhabits a cat."

Her attempt at humor failed.

"Go on, Mrs. Dahl. So you went downstairs ..."

Maggie did not mention the gun. She wasn't at risk of being charged for possessing it, but she thought it best not to add that particular color to the scene. She'd also not said anything to him about her meeting with Dahlia Getty. She was still trying to piece everything together. She would tell Hoyt about these things when the time came. For now she was only there to talk about a stranger coming into her house.

Hoyt thought a moment and set the pen down.

"Mrs. Dahl ..."

"Maggie."

"*Mrs. Dahl,*" he said, "why would someone come into your home and remain downstairs? Is there something they might be looking for?

Like the half million dollars we didn't find in Alice's house? Maggie thought.

"And how did they get in? You told me you didn't lock your doors."

"David made me lock them," Maggie said. "I fell back into the habit of leaving them unlocked when he died. But after Alice came into my house, I locked them again. I know I did."

Hoyt wrote several sentences, then put his pen down and eased back into his chair.

"From what you've told me, nothing was taken. The door was open. Maybe you left it unlocked, maybe you didn't. Maybe a strong wind invited itself into your house."

Maggie started to protest. Hoyt put his hand up, stopping her.

"Whatever happened, you were unharmed. The intruder left rather than confront you. It could have been a homeless person looking for food ..."

"In *Lambertville*? I didn't know there were any homeless people here."

"You'd be surprised. There are also people who wander at night, they take sleeping pills and suddenly they've walked around for an hour without remembering it. It happens."

Maggie was disheartened in the extreme. She'd come looking for support and advice, and instead she'd run headlong into a skeptic. If there was some connection between Alice's killing and her middle-of-the-night intruder, he wasn't making it.

"What if it's related?" she asked.

He stared at her. "Related to what?"

She sensed he knew what she meant but had not wanted to give it credibility.

"Alice's murder. What if he was trying to tell me something?"

"Assuming it's a man, and that it's *one* man," he said impatiently.

Maggie knew then he'd been humoring her and had decided to stop.

"Maybe it was a band of thieves," he said. "Maybe it was a tribe of some kind, men, women, children, pets."

"You don't need to mock me."

"One, I'm not mocking you. I'm illustrating how irrational you're being. Two, I'm conducting an active investigation into the death of Alice Drapier and I don't need these distractions. You broke into her house—"

"I had a key!"

"That is beside the point. You did not have her permission, and she didn't give it to you from the grave. I let that slide, which was against my better judgment and very much against department protocol. And now you're convinced her killer is trying to scare you off. From what, Mrs. Dahl? Is there something you're not telling me that has this man after you?"

Maggie clenched her teeth. "No," she lied. "Nothing that I'm aware of. Maybe he's afraid I know who he is. Maybe he thinks I saw him."

Hoyt looked at his watch. "I'm late for an interview," he said. "I don't mean to be rude, but if you'd like to file a report you can see the desk sergeant. In any event, I need to end this conversation. I'm a punctual man."

"Fine," Maggie said. She reached down and picked her purse up from the floor. "I appreciate your time."

"So are you going to file a report?" he asked.

Maggie was already formulating her next move. Hoyt was not on her side—at least not yet—and it might be best to pull back, to let the whole intruder business slide for now. She'd decided while being mildly reprimanded by the sergeant that she was right—whoever killed Alice was telling her to stay away. And that she would not do.

"I think you're correct, Sergeant Hoyt," she said as he led her to the door. "I was sleeping, I was exhausted, I probably imagined it all."

"I'm not saying you did."

"And you're not saying I *didn't*. I'd rather let it sit, maybe it was a figment of a very tired imagination. I'm sorry to take up your time."

"That's perfectly fine, I'm happy to listen. Just do me a favor …"

"What's that?" Maggie asked as she stepped into the hallway.

"Tell me you're coming the next time. And get your locks replaced."

"Done," said Maggie. "The locksmith came first thing this morning."

"Good. Don't hand keys out to anyone you don't trust, and you should be fine."

This time he smiled.

Maggie thanked him and shook his hand, then headed up the hallway toward the reception area. The next time she came to him with something, she would have to bring proof.

CHAPTER Twenty-One

FOR A STORE THAT HADN'T opened yet, Dahl House Jams and Specialties was bustling. Maggie arrived there after her interview with Sergeant Hoyt, finding the small storefront crowded with her own staff. Peter Stapley had come over with Sybil to deliver three cases of jams they'd prepared the night before, leaving Sybil's cousin Gloria to tend to the factory by herself for an hour or so. Janice was there, too, going over invoices and paperwork. The opening of a store, as Maggie had discovered since David's death, required a Herculean effort and all the help she could get.

To Maggie's surprise, Gerri had come over from the house, checking shelves and displays, moving jars and custom items a quarter inch or so as she tried to line everything up in her version of perfection.

"So how did it go with Tom Brightmore?" Maggie asked her sister when she got settled in.

"Well enough for a repeat," Gerri replied. Glancing at the others, she added, "I'll tell you about it later."

"Oh, sure," said Maggie, understanding her sister's need for privacy when it came to discussing something so personal.

"Everything's paid," Janice said from behind the front counter. She had a stack of invoices in her hand. She was frowning.

Seeing her expression, Maggie asked "Is that a bad thing?"

Janice sighed. She'd run a business before. More

than one, in fact, having been a freelance bookkeeper for several years as well as managing the finances for her husband's catering company. (She wasn't a "food person" herself, as she'd explained to Maggie; she was happy to do the books for Joe but she had no interest in cooking for a living—that was his ambition, and one he'd done successfully for the past six years).

"Pay on the terms, Maggie, I've told you that before. If it's Net 30, you pay in thirty days. There's no reason to pay them sooner, and you need the cash flow."

"But I've never carried debt in my life," Maggie said, defending her approach to debt. "David and I paid everything immediately. We didn't even have a mortgage, Janice."

"You didn't have a business then, either," said the resolute and indispensable assistant. "You have to be prepared to lose money the first six months. That means you *need* the money you have on hand. People juggle finances all the time, it's the way the world works. It's certainly the way the business world works. So get used to it, and stop paying invoices the minute you lay eyes on them."

"Fine," Maggie said. She trusted Janice. David had trusted her, too, and he would surely have taken her advice. It was just hard for Maggie to change habits she'd had for so many years.

"What else can we do for you, Boss?"

Maggie turned around, startled. The voice was Peter's. He was standing behind her, hands on hips, wiping sweat from his forehead. Maggie could see Sybil sweeping the floor in the small office area where she'd put a desk, computer and two filing cabinets.

"Tell me you're not cleaning this place, Peter," Maggie said, nodding toward Sybil in the background.

"Just a little."

"No, that's not your job and I don't want you bothering with it. You and the ladies are my chefs, my master jam and jelly crew. I need you doing that, not mopping floors or sweeping offices."

"We clean the factory, Boss."

"That's not the same. I never asked you to take on work at the store and I won't. If you or Gloria or Sybil want to work here part time, we can discuss it, but I won't burden you with work I didn't hire you for. I wouldn't ask you to pick up my dry cleaning, either."

"She has me for that!" Janice piped up, smiling from the cash register.

"She's being clever," said Maggie. "I've never asked Janice to run errands and I never will. Now please, you and Sybil go back to the factory and do what you do best."

"Sure thing, Boss," Peter said. He waved at Sybil. She set her broom against the office doorframe and followed him toward the door.

"We'll see you later," Sybil said to Maggie. When Peter had gone outside before her, she turned to Maggie and said in a lowered voice, "Anything that keeps him busy, Mrs. Dahl. Remember that. Even mopping floors."

Maggie was surprised by the comment and felt foolish for not having thought of it herself. Peter had been in a fragile state for a long time and might remain that way for years to come. She knew something about fragile states, having survived David's death with a diminished will to continue, but survive she had. Peter, too, had managed to keep going, but as Sybil had just gently reminded her, he still needed help. He needed to be busy.

"Thank you for reminding me," Maggie said to Sybil. "I'll see you at the factory later."

Sybil gave them all a wave and headed out to Peter's truck where he was already waiting behind the steering wheel.

The three women spent the next hour getting the store ready, with Janice focusing on paperwork and an ad Maggie wanted placed for part-time help. She knew she could count on Janice juggling jobs between the factory and working at the store, but she'd wanted to find someone outside her immediate circle who would be content helping out on a part-time schedule. Janice Cleary had greater ambitions, that was evident.

The more Maggie had anticipated running Dahl House Jams and Specialties, the closer she'd become to Janice as both a friend and a working partner. She'd even considered offering Janice a share of the business. She knew the Clearys weren't well off. Joe's catering business was successful, but not wildly so. Maggie had hired him to cater the store opening. She knew from talking to Janice that he had three employees who worked other jobs as well, and that his plans to expand had been put on hold until business picked up—never a certainty. She wouldn't ask Janice to pay her any substantial amount of money, but instead had thought of offering a stake in the company in exchange for Janice's time and labor. It was something she planned to talk to Janice about once they got through the store opening.

Her thoughts about Gerri were a different matter. Gerri had asked Maggie about working at the store, at least until she got acclimated to her new life in

Lambertville. Maggie was still not sure living together was a good idea, and working together might be a huge mistake. She'd even had fears about it with David. Being married to someone is not the same as running a business with them, and Maggie had known at least one couple in New York whose decision to undertake a business venture together spelled the end of their marriage. Apparently spending twenty-four hours a day with your spouse was not a recipe for a successful relationship.

"What are you thinking about?" Gerri asked. She'd been setting up the jams Peter and Sybil had delivered.

"How much I like those shelves," Maggie said. She was not going to get into a discussion about living arrangements or hiring decisions.

"I think they're great," Janice said. She was in the office now but could see into the main room. "You picked those out with David, yes?"

"That's correct," said Maggie. She and David had found the two shelves at a giant flea market outside of Lambertville. David had refinished them himself. They stood chest high on Maggie and each had five available shelves, perfect for displaying jams, jellies, and smaller custom tableware.

"I've been thinking about the walls," Maggie said, looking around the store.

"The walls?" asked Gerri. "What about the walls?"

"Decorating them, of course," Maggie replied. "There's nothing on them! We need paintings or photographs."

Janice had gotten up from the desk and was standing in the doorway. "How about old-timey ads, like from the 1950s, but selling jams and bread and that sort of thing?"

Maggie kept looking around at the room, thinking. "I'm not sure about that. I like the idea, but we're not, I don't know ..."

"Backward looking," offered Gerri.

"Yes, that's one way to put it. Those would be more appropriate to a vintage store or something like that. Dahl House Jams is comfortable, for sure, with a kind of Grandma vibe to it, but we have our eyes on the future."

"We have to," Janice said, nodding. "You're right. Old ads are great — for someone else."

"There's a gallery in town I've been wanting to visit," Maggie said. "Maybe there's something I can pick up there, a few pictures."

"Gallery as in 'art gallery'?" Janice asked. "Isn't that kind of expensive?"

"Let me guess," Gerri said. "You're talking about Valley Visions."

Maggie had told Gerri about Heather McGill and her art gallery the morning after her encounter with Dahlia Getty.

"That's the place," Maggie said.

"How about the flea market?" Janice said. "It's huge. We could get some real bargains there, nice things, too — paintings, or photographs."

"That's an excellent suggestion," said Maggie. "But I still want to take a look at Valley Visions. I'd like to support local artists if I can."

Maggie went behind the counter and got her purse from under the cash register. "As a matter of fact, let's walk over there now," she said to Gerri. "Janice can finish up here and we can grab some lunch after we stop at the gallery."

"Would you like me to come with you?" Janice

offered.

Maggie knew Janice was thinking about budgets, account balances, and saving Maggie from her own spending impulses. What she did not know was that Maggie had no intention of buying artwork. She was going to have a conversation with Heather McGill. She'd been thinking about how to start that conversation and decided today was as good a time as any.

"No, Janice, but thank you," she said. "I promise not to buy anything without showing you first!"

"Hey, it's your business. If you want a Picasso on the wall, go for it."

"If I had a Picasso I'd be retired," Maggie said. "Have some faith in me, Janice, I'm as money conscious as you are. We have to be. Dahl House Jams and Specialties will *not* fail, at least not from bad money management."

"We won't fail at all."

Maggie smiled. She knew she'd gotten lucky finding Janice, and she needed the comfort of her assistant's steady hand more than ever.

"Let's go," said Maggie, leading the way as she and Gerri left the store.

CHAPTER Twenty-Two

ONE OF THE FIRST THINGS Maggie and David had noticed about Lambertville was its artistic sensibility. It wasn't *artsy*, really, not in an artificial, pretentious way so evident in places like SoHo or small towns where painters and writers outnumbered regular people. Lambertville was creative without being forced about it. From the restaurants to the coffee shops, to the antique stores and art galleries, it all felt accessible, as if the artist on display was your aunt or the author signing books was your best friend from high school.

Maggie had been to the Valley Visions gallery, named for the Delaware River Valley they all lived in, without ever realizing who owned it. Valley Visions specialized in local artists, and the small storefront it was housed in offered paintings from names that might be familiar in the nearest diner or dress shop.

"Have you ever spoken to her?" Gerri asked. They were walking up Bridge Street from the car. Maggie had parked where there were no meters. An abundance of free parking was one of the advantages Lambertville had over New Hope.

"No," said Maggie. "I hadn't even connected the two until my conversation with Dahlia Getty. I don't know what Heather McGill looks like ... at least not to put a name to her, but I'm sure I've seen her around."

"Does she know we're coming?"

"No, and I want it that way. An element of surprise might help. She won't be expecting anyone to ask her about Alice Drapier's debt."

"Debt she now owns and will never recover."

"It makes her an unlikely suspect, don't you think?"

"I don't know," said Gerri, as they approached the gallery entrance. "If she was willing to buy Alice's debt from a loan shark, she might just be willing to bury a hammer in her skull."

Maggie thought that was improbable but didn't say anything. They'd arrived at the gallery and it was time to compose herself. She was about to attempt a conversation with a woman who may not be in a talkative mood.

The front of the gallery, like most storefronts, was composed of tall windows and an awning. Several paintings were on easels facing the street, so pedestrians and potential buyers could view them when they were strolling by.

"I like that," Gerri said, pointing at a landscape depicting the same bridge they could see two blocks away.

"The entire area lends itself to being painted and photographed," Maggie said. "I wouldn't call it breathtaking, to be honest, but it's very beautiful."

Maggie led them inside. Like most businesses of its kind, Valley Visions was quiet, as if talking above a whisper would offend the muses. There was classical music playing softly over a speaker mounted in one corner, but nothing else that might be considered noise.

A dozen paintings were displayed throughout the main area and in a second room they could see beyond the front desk. Behind the desk sat a tall, thin woman Maggie assumed was Heather McGill. She had seen her around, but had never asked anyone who she was. She had *not* seen her with her father, Chip, and she wondered why that was. Were they estranged? Or did they simply travel in different circles, given Heather's position as an art gallery owner and Chip's as a handyman with a drinking problem?

"Good morning, ladies," Heather said. She stood up from the chair, stepping around the small desk.

She would be called statuesque if people still used that word. Her hair was light brown and exceptionally long, pulled back and expertly braided in a tail that fell over her shoulder, down past her breast. She wore reading glasses she removed when she got up from the chair.

"Good morning," Maggie said. "I'm looking for Heather McGill."

"That would be me," Heather said. "I recognize you, by the way. I don't think we've met." She extended her hand.

Maggie returned the gesture, gently shaking hands, and said, "Maggie Dahl, and this is my sister Gerri."

Heather cocked her head a moment, thinking. "Yes, I remember now. You're the jam lady. I'm sorry about your husband."

"And I'm sorry we haven't met. Lambertville's not a big place."

"Big enough that we could pass each other on the street many times and never speak."

"Yes."

It was time to steer the conversation into riskier territory. Maggie had no idea how Heather would react but she had to find out.

"I'm the one who discovered Alice Drapier's body," Maggie said.

She saw a flicker in Heather's eyes, accompanied by a small twitch of the mouth.

Gerri, meanwhile, had left the two women alone, casually looking at the other paintings on display.

"That must have been terrible," Heather said. "But what does this have to do with me, or the gallery?"

Maggie decided it was best to just come out with it. Either Heather would tell her something, or she would go silent and ask them to leave.

"I was told by someone I believe that Alice was deeply in debt to a ... how can I say this? ..."

"Loan shark."

It was Maggie's turn to be surprised. "Yes, for lack of a better term."

"There is no other term, Mrs. Dahl. Alice owed money to someone, and I purchased the note. We can cut the nonsense and say that. That's why you're here, it must be."

Maggie was unable to tell if the McGill woman was expressing dislike for her or just being blunt.

"Yes, it is why I'm here. I'm trying to find out who killed Alice, or at least who would want to kill her, and that's led me to you."

Heather laughed, a sound that included a certain acidity. "And you think it was me?"

"I didn't say that."

"But you implied it."

"Actually, I didn't. But your father has done a lot of work for me and my late husband. You purchased Alice's debt. Father, daughter ... I'm just wondering if there's more than a familial connection there, something that needs to be looked at."

"Try the newspaper archives," Heather said. "Go back ten years. A girl disappeared here."

This was not at all what Maggie had expected. Suddenly Alice's murder, her debt, and the purchase of that debt were being connected to the disappearance of Lilly Stapley. Maggie knew exactly who Heather was talking about.

"The Stapley girl," she said. "Her father works for me."

"Small world," Heather said, this time with distinct bitterness.

"Small town. But what does Lilly Stapley's disappearance have to do with Alice Drapier?"

"Wrong question, Mrs. Dahl. You should ask what Lilly's disappearance has to do with my father."

Maggie's head was spinning.

"I'll ask it now, then," she said. The room suddenly seemed even more quiet. She sensed Gerri inching closer to them, pretending to look at a painting while eavesdropping on their conversation.

Heather stared at her and said, "Alice Drapier, who you seem to think was a good person, was the main source of a whisper campaign against my father."

Maggie was stunned. This wasn't just new information — it was shocking information.

"She thought he was the predator," Heather continued. "I don't know why. Maybe she owed him money for work he'd done and she didn't pay him. He could be aggressive about that kind of thing. Or maybe she'd come on to him — it wouldn't be the first time a lonely, married woman did that — and he'd rejected her. Whatever her reasons, she started telling people, in that small town 'I'm just saying' kind of way we have, that she thought my father had something to do with the Lilly Stapley kidnapping."

"Did he?" asked Maggie. It was an obvious question, and one she immediately regretted.

"Of course he didn't have anything to do with it!"

Heather snapped. "That didn't stop her from repeatedly suggesting he did. He always drank more than he should, but after that it was a long downward spiral, resulting in the broken man you see now. There, Mrs. Dahl. You have it. I bought her debt to keep her here."

"I didn't know she was leaving."

"There's a lot you don't know. Alice was planning to sell her house and leave town, cats and all. But she had to pay the piper first."

"The piper being you."

"Correct. The bank wouldn't give her a second mortgage, you see."

"But Dahlia Getty would."

"You're a sharp lady. Between her house payment, her gambling debt, and the money she now owed to me, Alice wasn't going anywhere. I wanted Alice here and miserable. I'd hoped that would be enough to kill her, but I would never do it myself."

The sound of the door opening drew their attention. Heather McGill, seeing a new visitor and a way to end the conversation, drew a smile to her face. "Welcome," she said over Maggie's shoulder, then to Maggie, "You can leave now."

Maggie had nothing else to say to her. She waved at Gerri, who'd turned to watch them. "We'll do that. Thank you for the information."

"It wasn't much." Leaning in and whispering, she added, "I hope you find Alice's killer, not because I'm sorry she's dead, but because Lambertville doesn't need another unsolved murder."

"You think Lilly Stapley was killed?"

Heather shrugged. "It's been ten years. I wouldn't want those odds."

Maggie nodded. Gerri joined her at the desk, and together they left Valley Visions as quietly as they'd arrived.

CHAPTER Twenty-Three

HALLOWEEN WAS FAST APPROACHING AND Maggie was feeling the pressures that had accumulated in her life the past six months. David was gone forever, leaving her with a home, a business, and an ocean of grief she would be navigating for years to come. Her sister was living in their house. Maggie had admitted to herself that it was still very much *David's* house, too, and she wasn't sure how he would feel about Gerri planting her flag in an upstairs bedroom. The factory was keeping up with its orders, though another large one would strain it to its limits, and the store was about to open.

She regretted not opening Dahl House Jams and Specialties a week sooner. Halloween was in full swing in Lambertville, and she saw every gawker strolling the streets taking selfies and photos of the outlandish decorations as a lost sale. *I could have sold a jam to that one,* she thought, staring out the front window at the passersby. *I could have sold a butter dish to them.*

"What are you thinking?" Gerri asked.

They'd headed to the store after Maggie's conversation with Heather McGill. Maggie didn't have a particular reason to go there—everything was in order and she expected to have the grand opening in two days as planned—but it had become a safe place for her. David was here. He was at the factory, too, and in every room of her house. She wanted to be where she felt his presence, and the store was still a quiet space.

"I was wishing it was over," Maggie replied.

"The murder investigation?"

"All of it. The house renovation. The store opening. The whole Alice thing, for sure. I don't know why I care. And frankly, the more I learn about Alice Drapier, the less I think I *should* care. She wasn't a nice person."

"No, but she was your neighbor. If you hadn't pursued this, the things you liked about her would be all you know. So she had secrets. We all do."

The statement made Maggie think. Did she have secrets? Her fondness for shooting, her trips to the firing range with David—she supposed those could be called secrets. But she had never done something she'd kept from others out of guilt. She didn't have *dark* secrets.

"Do you have secrets?" Maggie asked.

"If I told you, they wouldn't be secrets anymore, would they?" Gerri winked at Maggie. "So what's next?"

"I'm not sure. I believe Chip is at the center of it, but I can't imagine how."

"The alcoholic handyman did it?"

Maggie shrugged. "I just cannot see Chip hurting anyone."

"But you could see him breaking into your house."

"I don't know, Gerri! I certainly can't see him bringing a hammer down on Alice's head. But I couldn't see Alice owing money to a loan shark or spreading vicious rumors about Chip, either. You're the one who said we all have secrets."

"Yes, and some of them are worth killing for, don't forget that."

Gerri went to a coatrack in the corner and slid her jacket off the hook.

"If you'll excuse me, I'm heading home to change for dinner."

"Oh," said Maggie, "I thought I'd make something …"

Smiling, Gerri stopped her. "No need. I'm dining with Tom again."

Maggie knew her sister was very much an adult, and that her choices were none of her business as long as they did not involve her home, but she had great misgivings about Gerri developing a romantic life less than a week after moving in.

"What exactly are you looking for?"

Gerri stared at Maggie, annoyance flashing in her eyes. "I'm not looking for anything. I have my own gold, if that's what you're implying."

"I didn't mean that, Gerri."

"Companionship, then. Let's just say I'm looking for new friends in a new place, and Tom Brightmore promises to be one of them."

Maggie nodded: well enough. Gerri slipped her coat on and walked to the door. She turned back to Maggie and said, "Don't worry about me. He's a nice man, younger, I know, but who doesn't deserve that? It's dinner, for godsake, Maggie. Life has crapped on me a few times, let me just enjoy this."

Maggie knew she was right. Gerri had had more than her share of hardships, obstacles and abandonments. She was a tough one, and she could handle herself. It was time for Maggie to let her.

"Have a good time," Maggie said. "I might see you at the house before you leave, I might not. I'm stopping at the factory first."

"Say hello to the crew," Gerri said. Then she left and closed the door behind her, the bell tinkling as the door shut.

Maggie watched her walk up the street. She wished she'd left Alice's murder to the police, or, better yet, that she'd never found Alice's body. But it was too late now. She'd gone down a path she would not veer from. What she discovered at the end of it could be life, death, or none of the above. She thought about the gun in the night stand.

She awoke with a start. It had not been a dream that disturbed her this time. She hadn't dreamed at all. The hours she'd been asleep—for the first thing she did when her eyes opened was look at the nightstand clock and see it was 1:00 a.m.—had been mercifully free of thoughts and images. A black void, the kind in which she finally rested and that she had enjoyed so few of the past six months.

So what had made her wake up? Checks was sitting on the edge of the bed, staring at the door. Not curled, but sitting, a silent feline sentinel in the night. Had the intruder returned? Maggie listened for any sounds, even as she reached over the edge of the bed and opened the drawer where the gun was. She let her fingers caress it, but she did not take it out. Something told her no one was in the house, there was no reason to arm herself.

Leaving the drawer open just in case, she slipped out of bed and tiptoed to the door. Checks remained on the bedspread, letting Maggie take the lead in whatever was about to happen. She eased into the door frame and stuck her head out, listening. Still no sounds. She looked left, then right. And she saw it: Gerri's bedroom door was open. The TV light was not casting shadows on the floor. Gerri wasn't home.

"Really?" Maggie said to herself, as she headed down the hallway to her sister's room.

Checks jumped off the bed and followed.

Maggie reached Gerri's room and looked in. The bed was still made. Everything was exactly as it had been when Gerri went out for her dinner date.

Looking down at Checks, who was now at her feet, Maggie said, "What are we going to do with my sister, Checks? I'm open to suggestions."

Knowing she had the choice of waiting up for Gerri or returning to bed, Maggie reminded herself that her sister was forty-nine years old and perfectly capable of taking care of herself, even without a gun.

She went back to bed, hoping that the void of rest and peace was still there when she got back to sleep. She'd had enough for one day—for one lifetime—and she needed the bliss of unconsciousness. She would deal with her sister in the light of day.

Leaving the nightstand drawer open, Maggie pulled the bedspread over her. She reached out and petted Checks. The cat curled into a ball this time, still staring at the door but letting Maggie know it was safe to close her eyes again … for now.

DAY 5

"Those who'll play with cats must expect to be scratched."

– Miguel de Cervantes

CHAPTER Twenty-Four

NEITHER WOMAN SPOKE. MAGGIE WAS making breakfast for herself while Gerri sat at the kitchen table drinking her first cup of coffee. Maggie had been up for two hours and was dressed for the day; Gerri had been up for two minutes, from the look of it, and had chosen not to initiate a conversation.

Buttering her toast, Maggie said, "So, sister ... late night? Or did you just get home?"

"Cute," said Gerri. "You know perfectly well I was out late. You probably stayed up until you heard me come in."

"I did no such thing. I'll admit I knew you were out. Something woke me up around one."

"Not an intruder again, I hope."

"No. It was nothing. I just woke up. I checked things out and saw you hadn't come home yet."

Gerri took another sip of coffee. "I'm forty-nine years old, Maggie. Fifty in December. I think I can stay out past my curfew."

Maggie brought her plate over and sat across from Gerri.

"You don't have a curfew. I just worry about you." After a moment, she added, "So how did it go? Did you stay the night?"

Gerri smiled. "You mean did we sleep together? I do wish we could do away with euphemisms. The question is, did we have sex? The answer is, no. Not this time."

159

Maggie's eyebrow arched. "But maybe next time?"

"I'm hoping soon. I could use a little man action. Anything would be better than my last husband. Make that all three of them."

Maggie waited a moment for Gerri to continue. When she didn't, Maggie said, "Fair enough. If you don't want to talk about it …"

"I do! Just not right now. I'd rather savor it a little while."

"*Savor*? Oh, my."

"We had a wonderful time. We talked. That's all we did, but we *really* talked. Two divorcees spending an evening together getting to know each other. And that's all I feel like saying for now. What are you up to today?"

Maggie offered Gerri a piece of toast. She took it and nibbled, waiting for Maggie to answer.

"Chip's coming over to do more work and I want to have a conversation with him."

"About killing Alice Drapier?"

"I'd never be that blunt," said Maggie. "I want to carefully ask him about a key he had made."

Surprised, Gerri said, "You think he secretly had a key made to this house?"

"It wasn't a secret. David wanted him to have one so he could work on renovation projects while we were out."

Gerri grew serious. "It was him."

"I don't know that. I want to think it *wasn't* him, but he's connected to all this and I just want to put some feelers out, that's all."

"You're living dangerously, Maggie. Don't the neighbors always say, 'He was such a nice man!' when someone gets arrested for killing his family? If murderers looked the part, we'd be much safer. I can't stop you, but I can tell you to be careful."

"I could say the same to you, staying out half the night with a man you just met."

Finished with her toast, Gerri set half the slice back on Maggie's plate.

"Touché. Let's both be careful. And I promise to tell you all about Tom Brightmore and our enchanting evening in his *living* room. Now if you'll excuse me, I need to properly get up for the day."

Gerri left the table and headed out of the kitchen. Turning around in the doorway, she said, "The bathroom light's out, by the way. The one over the sink."

"I'll go to Davies Hardware this afternoon and get a replacement. Can you see well enough until then?"

"Yes," Gerri replied. "I only needed to look my best last night."

She waved bye-bye to Maggie and headed upstairs.

Maggie glanced at the clock: Chip McGill was set to arrive in twenty minutes. She planned on asking him a question or two and hoped he gave the right answers.

Maggie had never hovered over Chip when he was working. For one thing, she would find it annoying if someone stood over her at her job—her bosses had done it enough over the years—and for another, Chip knew what he was doing. He may have a drinking problem, but when it came to home repairs, painting, and fixing fireplaces, he was as good as anyone.

Her discomfort was heightened by knowing what she'd learned from Chip's daughter. Watching him scrape the mantle on her fireplace, she had a new respect for the man. He'd been accused of abducting a young girl, condemned by gossip for something he didn't do. Alice's whisper campaign had ruined his marriage and embittered his daughter to the point of vengeance. But was the purchase of Alice's debt the only revenge exacted?

Chip didn't seem to notice Maggie stalling in the living room while he worked on the fireplace. She usually made small talk with him, then went on about her day. He didn't see her when she casually walked over to his toolbox and peered into it. He was oblivious to her look of curiosity when she saw a new hammer among his tools, complete with the fresh price tag on it.

Where is the old hammer? thought Maggie. She'd never paid any attention to Chip's toolbox before. It was like any toolbox she'd ever seen, dented, scraped, and filled with tools sticking out every which way. But the hammer was on top, and it was new. Surely, she thought, the old one had not been left on Alice Drapier's kitchen floor. Even a drunken Chip McGill would not be that sloppy in the commitment of murder.

Maggie cleared her throat, getting Chip's attention. He was on his hands and knees now, prying tile loose from the floor around the fireplace.

Turning to her, Chip said, "I didn't see you there, Mrs. Dahl. Sorry. Did you need something?"

Pushing thoughts of the hammer away, Maggie said, "I wanted to ask you about the house key David had you make for yourself."

Chip cocked his head: this was an odd question. "What about it?"

Lying, Maggie said, "Did he ever pay you for it? For having the key made?"

She felt ridiculous. David had been dead for six

months. The key would have cost a couple dollars. And *now* she was asking about it? She hoped Chip would write it off as an afterthought from a grieving widow.

Chip said, "Mr. Dahl always gave me money when I needed to buy things for the house. And besides, I didn't keep the key."

Maggie stared at him a moment. "I don't understand."

"I had it made because he asked me to," Chip explained. "But I gave the key — and the change — to Mr. Dahl."

Chip was clearly uncomfortable. He sat up on his haunches and continued.

"I don't want keys to people's houses. It can lead to … misunderstandings."

"Did you have a key to the Stapley's house?" Maggie asked, surprised she'd blurted it out.

Looking as if someone had slapped him, Chip took a deep breath and replied, "Yes, Mrs. Dahl, I did. I did handy work for Mrs. Stapley now and then. The police asked me that same question, several times, even though the child wasn't taken from her home. I had nothing to do with the Stapley girl's disappearance, and I have never kept a key to anyone's house since. If someone wants me to do work for them, they can meet me at the front door, or the back, doesn't matter to me. But I won't be using a key. Now if you'll excuse me …"

Maggie had flushed hot with shame. She hadn't meant to upset Chip, only to pry carefully. She's failed spectacularly. She started to leave the room, leaving him to his anger.

"We had an affair," Chip said over his shoulder, stopping Maggie.

She turned back, listening.

Without facing her again, Chip said, "Alice and me. It went on for a few months, that's all. But she wasn't who I thought she was. She wanted … I don't know, really. Everything. Me to leave my wife. Her to leave her husband. It was crazy."

Maybe I should have called her Crazy Alice after all, Maggie thought.

"I said that was not going to happen, and she hated me for it. *Really* hated me. But what she did, the things she said when Lilly Stapley went missing …"

Maggie looked at Chip. His back was to her, but she saw him wipe away a tear—whether of rage or sorrow she couldn't tell.

"You don't need to say anymore," Maggie said. "I'm so sorry I brought this up. I'll leave you alone, Chip."

He nodded, maybe in thanks, maybe in agreement she should go. He did not speak again.

Maggie headed upstairs, still burning with guilt— but not enough to forget the new hammer in the toolbox, or Chip's claim to have given the duplicate key back to David.

Once in her bedroom, she went to the jewelry box David had used as a catchall drawer, his place to put things he didn't want to lose—including spare keys. He'd believed in having an extra set of everything. She stood at the dresser, reflecting on how long it had been since she'd opened this box. Since just after his death? Before it? Had she *ever* opened it?

She reached out slowly, as if the lid would burn her fingers. She gently lifted it up, and there it was: the spare key to the house, in a small compartment on top of other spare keys, some that she recognized and some she'd never known existed. *What did they unlock?* she wondered. My sorrow? My loss?

Leaving the key where she'd found it, she closed the jewelry box and left the room.

If you can have one key made, you can have two.

The thought struck her as she headed downstairs. If her discoveries about Alice had taught her anything, it was to remember that appearances can be deceiving. Just as her neighbor had been more complicated than she had ever imagined, so, too, might Chip McGill be.

She glanced at him, still working on the fireplace, as she left the house.

CHAPTER Twenty-Five

SERGEANT HOYT DID NOT INVITE Maggie to the conference room this time. He met her in the lobby when she arrived unannounced and sat beside her in the waiting area, his impatience evident.

"The first thing we examined was the hammer," he explained. "It's called a murder weapon."

Maggie had told him about Chip McGill's new hammer, speculating that the one it replaced had been used to kill Alice.

Hoyt sighed loudly. "Did you think that wouldn't occur to us? There were no fingerprints on the handle, which is none of your business, by the way, but I'm telling you anyway."

"So it could be Chip's!"

"It could be anyone's, Mrs. Dahl. A murderer clever enough to get a body back into a house without anyone seeing him is probably going to make sure he doesn't leave incriminating evidence. We've spoken to Chip. He replaces hammers now and then, he's a handyman. Again, this is none of your business, but he's not a person of interest in this. Did you want him to be?"

Maggie glanced out the window, wishing she hadn't come here. She'd managed to make a nuisance of herself while accomplishing nothing in the process. If the police didn't consider Chip a suspect, why should she?

Maggie said, "I don't know what I want or think,

Sergeant. I only know people are often not who we think they are."

She turned back to see Hoyt looking at her.

"Could you be more specific?" he asked.

"I thought Alice was just a distracted, sweet woman with a bunch of cats and too much time on her hands. I had no idea she had gambling debts—"

"Gambling debts?"

"—debts she couldn't repay without help."

Maggie did not tell him Alice got that help from a loan shark named Dahlia Getty, or that Getty sold the note to Heather McGill.

Continuing, Maggie said, "Or that she'd done something terrible to Chip McGill."

This time Hoyt took notice.

Seeing his expression, Maggie said, "You knew about Alice and her whisper campaign against Chip?"

"Yes, I knew about it. I was a rookie when Lilly Stapley disappeared. As a matter of fact, I was the first officer who showed up when Melissa Stapley called to say her daughter had vanished off the street."

Maggie could tell it was a sensitive subject for him and wondered if she'd made a mistake bringing it up.

"If Chip McGill was going to kill Alice Drapier for ruining his life, I don't think he would wait ten years to do it. I told you, he's not a person of interest. He has an alibi, which, like too much I've said, is none of your business and will remain that way."

Hoyt stood up, ending a conversation he'd clearly not wanted to have.

"I really have things to do, Mrs. Dahl."

Maggie got up from her chair, flustered and unsure what to do. "I'm sorry for wasting your time," she said.

Hoyt softened slightly. She had not spoken with any bitterness, her apology sincere.

He took her hand in more of a clasp than a shake and said, "We will find who did this, I'm sure of it."

"But you're not promising."

"I learned long ago in this profession not to make many promises. I once promised a mother we would find her daughter, and you see how that turned out."

Maggie nodded. "Thank you, Sergeant. I won't bother you again ..."

"Unnecessarily," he said, finishing her sentence. He smiled.

Maggie let his hand go and headed out to her car.

CHAPTER Twenty-Six

SHE'D ONLY MEANT TO STOP at Davies Hardware for a lightbulb. When Maggie left the police station after another fruitless conversation with Sergeant Hoyt, she'd felt dispirited. He wasn't humoring her anymore and he had made it clear the hammer that killed Alice did not belong to Chip McGill. She asked herself how stupid could she be not to assume the police—the *police*!—would examine the hammer first. If the killer had left fingerprints on it, they would have made an arrest by now. And Hoyt, of all people, would have thought immediately of McGill. He knew the history the handyman shared with Alice Drapier. He may not have known about the affair, but he certainly knew about the damage Alice had done with her deliberate rumors and veiled accusations.

Maggie was processing it all, wondering how long she could keep this up, with the store opening just days away and a business to run, when she reached the hardware store. Situated on Bridge Street between a beloved neighborhood bookstore called the Booketeria and Beverly Jewelers, Davies Hardware had been a fixture in town for decades. Cal Davies, the owner, took the business over from his late father and had worked there since he was a teenager. Everyone knew Cal, and Cal knew everyone.

The place smelled like a hardware store. Maggie had loved that smell since she was a child and her father had taken her with him to the local hardware store in their Brooklyn Heights neighborhood. It was hard to define, an intoxicating mix of plastic, chemicals, tools, wood … all blended into a fragrance unique to this type of business. You wouldn't smell it anywhere else.

She heard a distinctive whistling that reminded her of a tune she couldn't name. Light, cheerful, but unfamiliar.

"Morning, Mrs. Dahl," Cal said, glancing up from the front counter. The whistling had come from him, and stopped when he greeted her. He wore half-glasses and was examining a piece of paper a man had given him. It looked to be a list of supplies. The customer, his back to Maggie, glanced around briefly and nodded hello.

"Good morning," Maggie replied.

"I'll be right with you."

Maggie said, "Take your time," and walked past the counter. She figured she could browse while she waited for Cal. She might even find the light bulb on her own.

She heard Cal talking softly to the man at the counter. She walked slowly down a row of painting supplies — brushes, painter's tape, plastic tarps and rolling pans. She turned at the end of the aisle, headed back toward the front of the store and found herself looking at a section of hammers. She'd never known hammers came in such a variety: ball-peen hammers, framing hammers, upholstery hammers … and claw hammers. Right there in front of her. Not only the same *type* of hammer that had killed Alice, but the same brand.

Maggie reached out and took the hammer off the wall rack. She hadn't touched the hammer in Alice's kitchen, but she had seen it up close and she would swear the one in her hand was exactly the same. It had a price sticker and a Davies Hardware decal on the handle, but it was identical to both the hammer resting next to Alice's head and the one she'd seen in Chip McGill's toolbox that morning.

"May I help you?"

Maggie almost dropped the hammer on the floor. She had not heard Cal walk up to her, and the sound of his voice startled her. She turned to see him smiling at her. It was the first time she noticed his blue smock, with the store's name stitched over one breast and his own over the other. It made her wonder if there were any other employees, any other names stitched onto Davies Hardware smocks.

Putting the hammer back on the wall, Maggie said, "I was just looking for a lightbulb."

"In the hammer section?"

That smile again, which Maggie observed did not extend to his eyes.

"I was thinking of getting one for Chip McGill. He's working on our house — *my* house."

His expression changed to one of feigned compassion. "It's okay, Mrs. Dahl. I lost my wife fifteen years ago and I still say 'our.' People say it takes time. I say time has nothing to do with it."

"Right. Well, I was looking for a replacement light bulb for one of my bathrooms."

"I'm sure I have what you're looking for," said Cal. "Two aisles over."

Leading the way, Cal walked Maggie to an aisle that held any lightbulb she might need. And, as Cal told her, "If I don't have it, I'll order it. That's the Davies Hardware way."

She imagined him having a Davies Hardware

mission statement somewhere, with a set of Davies Hardware principles and Davies Hardware promises. The more she was alone with the man in his store, the more she wanted to position herself near the door.

As she was paying for her lightbulb, she saw a key-making machine behind the counter. She knew most people had keys made at hardware stores, especially in places like Lambertville. The local hardware store, like the barbershop, diner, and, once upon a time, Post Office, was a community center as well. Women kept up with each other at the salon, and men gossiped at the hardware store, even if they didn't call it gossiping.

"By the way," Maggie said, sliding her credit card back into her wallet. "Chip had a key made for my husband. It's been over six months so I don't expect you to remember this, but ..."

"Oh, I remember," Cal said, surprising her. "It was unusual for Chip to have a house key made. He hadn't done that for some time."

Maggie remembered the handyman's words, that he had no interest in having a key to anyone's home. It would be noticeable for him to make an exception. She was relieved when Davies used the singular. She also felt silly and a little ashamed.

"I assumed the keys were spares for you and Mr. Dahl."

The keys. Plural. More than one.

Maggie stared at him. "Keys?" she asked.

"Yes. He had two made, as I recall. Like I said, it's not something I've seen Chip do in a long time. He lives upstairs here, you know, in one of the apartments."

Maggie glanced at the ceiling, as if she could see through it into Chip's living room.

"Yes, I know. I was there once to pay him."

"What really made me remember it, though, was the receipt."

Maggie looked at him. "What about the receipt?"

"He wanted two, one for each of the duplicate keys. But Chip's a funny man, I assumed it had something to do with his bookkeeping."

"Yes," said Maggie, "I would assume that, too. I'm sure it did. I'll have to look at home and see if my husband kept both receipts."

She knew already there would not be two receipts.

"Anything else for you, Mrs. Dahl?" asked Cal.

Another customer came in, sparing Maggie any further awkward conversation.

"No," she said. "I'm good for today. Thanks for your help."

"It's the Davies Hardware way," he said, waving past her at the man who'd just entered.

"Of course it is," said Maggie.

She picked up the bag holding her new lightbulb, gave Cal Davies a final smile, and hurried out of the store.

CHAPTER Twenty-Seven

"WHY WOULD HE WANT A key to your house?"

Gerri asked her sister the obvious question. They were at Dahl House Jams and Specialties stringing crepe along the ceiling and putting up decorations for the opening. Maggie had recounted her trip to the hardware store and what Cal Davies had told her. She had to admit it made no sense—at least not immediately.

"I've been asking myself that for the past hour," said Maggie, standing on a ladder. "Help me with the streamers, will you?"

"Don't overdo it. It's a specialty shop, not a toy store."

Maggie had never opened a business before. She'd been fretting for weeks about how to do it. She'd asked around, talking to other shop owners, each of whom had their own ideas. She concluded it was mostly trial and error, though the error could be ruinous. Free food, tasteful party decorations, samples of her Dahl House Jams, and endless schmoozing—those would make up her recipe for success. Flyers had gone up around town, handed out by Janice and the factory crew. Invitations had been sent to select invitees who were encouraged to spread the word and bring as many friends as would come along. And an article was scheduled to run in the Hunterdon County Democrat, complete with an interview. The young reporter from the paper, a man named Dan Higgins, had set up an appointment with

Maggie for two weeks after the opening. By then she hoped to have good news about the store's smashing launch.

Gerri stood by the ladder, handing Maggie another streamer to tape up.

Maggie said, "It could be a fetish."

"The streamers?"

"The key!"

"You mean, like he collects them? Has sex with them?"

"Not that kind of fetish. How would you have sex with a key, anyway? Where would you put it? Don't answer that! No. I mean maybe he secretly has keys made to people's homes ..."

"While denying he has keys to anyone's home! Very clever."

"Then he sneaks into houses in the middle of the night for the thrill of it."

Shaking her head, Gerri said, "I don't believe in coincidence. This intruder came into the house just when you're sticking your nose where it could get broken."

"Into Alice Drapier's murder."

"Yes. I don't think it's an accident of timing."

"Neither do I."

Maggie descended the ladder. She stood and looked around at the room. They'd done about as much decorating as they could without turning a tasteful opening into something cheap and gaudy. On the other hand, she knew kids liked balloons, streamers, and especially jam. She wanted the store to appeal to people's children as well. Nobody says no to their kids — it was a strategic decision.

"I think I need to have another conversation," said

Maggie.

"With Chip McGill? *Again*? He's lying. He's not going to suddenly admit it."

"You're right. That's why I'm not going to talk to him. I'm going to talk to his daughter. She was very forthcoming."

"Blithely so. Have you considered she might be lying, too?"

"Maybe. She doesn't seem to care who knows what. I like that about her. If she'd killed Alice, she'd just admit it and shrug."

Gerri folded the ladder and leaned it against the wall.

"And you think she knows about her father's secret key making."

"Probably not, but she could find out more easily than I could."

"She has absolutely no reason to help you."

"Oh, I disagree. She has every reason to help me. If her father is an innocent man, she'll want to prove that."

"I'll go with you," Gerri said.

"No, not this time. I think Heather might be more comfortable if I go alone."

"Have it your way. But you might stop at home and get that gun."

"Very funny," said Maggie. "I'm not shooting anyone in an art gallery."

She would not get the gun, even if it had been a serious suggestion. She hoped a time never came when she really needed it.

CHAPTER Twenty-Eight

MAGGIE LEFT HER CAR IN front of Dahl House Jams and walked to the Valley Visions gallery. The walk was less than ten minutes but it would give her time to think. She could not imagine why Chip would secretly copy a key to their house. If it wasn't something he was in the habit of doing, a sort of perverse hobby, then it was specific to their house. But that was absurd, she thought. Why on earth would he want secret entry to her home?

There was nothing of particular interest in the house's history. David had noticed it for sale when they'd taken their first long stroll through town. He'd wanted to see the side streets, believing that was how you got to know the real character of a place. The main thoroughfares were nice enough with their art galleries, shops and restaurants. But the people who inhabited communities like Lambertville lived, for the most part, off to the side. So they'd walked casually down one side street and back on another, noting the street names and marveling at many of the houses. Even small houses here have a sense of belonging to them, of comfort, as if they, too, are longtime residents in a place they call home.

Then they came to Delevan Street. As they headed back toward their car four blocks away, David noticed the old house for sale. It looked as if it had been unoccupied for some time, and in need of repair even longer.

"What do you think?" he'd asked, stopping in front of the house.

"What do I think about what?"

"This house."

"I think it looks like it needs a lot of work. And how do you keep something that big warm in the winter? The heating bills must be enormous!"

Maggie was not initially impressed with the house and had wanted to forget it. They hadn't really discussed this part of any move. She'd seen them buying a condo, not a hundred-fifty-year-old structure with warped floors and a crumbling fireplace.

Two months later they were living in the house, and David had hired Chip McGill to help him restore it. David's grand vision for their home was far from realized when he died. Maggie wasn't sure it would ever be what David imagined it, but she would at least finish with the basics. Selling was not an option at this point. The house was too much a part of their dreams.

But why would Chip want a key to this house? Had he played there as a child? Had he done something only he knew about, there in the spacious living room? Or maybe he'd dated a girl who'd lived there and he had wanted to relive whatever moments he'd had with her alone when Maggie and David were gone. Or maybe he was just a thief. He was certainly an intruder. Maggie was convinced Chip was the one who'd come into her home and startled the ever-watchful cat. Only someone with a key could have done that. She'd had the locks changed, so it wouldn't happen again. But it was what happened in the past that concerned her now.

Heather was at the front desk using her smartphone

when she heard the door open. She was not surprised to see Maggie enter her galley again. She was also not pleased and made no attempt to hide her displeasure.

There was no one else there—Maggie had long observed that art and photography galleries were often empty—which gave her the opportunity she'd hoped for to speak with Heather alone and uninterrupted.

Maggie said, "Good afternoon," and closed the door behind her, glancing out the front window as to make sure no one else was coming in.

Heather did not return the pleasantry. She also did not budge from her place behind the desk.

Walking up to her, Maggie said, "I was hoping we could speak a little more."

"About what, Mrs. Dahl? I told you everything I had to say. Some might think I told you too much."

"Because of the debt business with Alice?"

"Possibly. But holding someone's debt is not a crime. I never loaned her money, and I never collected payment, with or without interest." Finally getting up, while keeping the desk between them, she added, "If speaking will hurry this along, then fine. What did you want to talk about?"

This was the hard part for Maggie. She'd tried to sort it all out on the walk over from the store, but she was still not sure what it was she needed to know, or how to go about asking. She decided on the spot that a direct approach would be the best, especially with a woman as blunt as Heather McGill.

"I believe your father secretly had a key made to my house and I can't figure out why."

Heather stared at her as if Maggie had just suggested an asteroid was about to crash through the gallery window.

"Do you know how ridiculous that sounds?"

"I understand why you would think that ..."

"*I* would think that?" Heather was angry now. "*Anyone* would think that. Why on earth would my father want a key to your or anyone else's house? He stopped keeping keys to people's homes when all that Lilly Stapley business happened. The last thing he wants is a key to your home. You really are going off the rails with this, Mrs. Dahl."

"I have good reason to, Heather," said Maggie. She could see the woman bristle at being addressed by her name in such a casual way. "Ms. McGill," Maggie corrected. Someone broke into my home a few nights ago."

"And you think it was my father. But why would anyone with a key break in?"

Maggie chastised herself for not being clear. "No, I'm sorry, they didn't break in, they *came* in ... they intruded."

"Again, Mrs. Dahl, why would you think it was my father?"

Maggie hesitated. She did not want to bring Cal Davies into the conversation. What he'd told her seemed like important information she should keep to herself for the moment.

"I just do," said Maggie, avoiding any further explanation.

Heather shook her head sadly, as if the woman asking her to incriminate her own father was more troubled than Alice Drapier had been. Then, having a thought, she asked Maggie, "What night was this?"

"The night before last. Why?"

"You're sure about that?"

"Yes. Two nights ago, at three a.m. I looked at the

clock on my nightstand when I heard someone downstairs."

"I see." Heather sighed, offering a sad expression. "It could not have been my father."

Thinking Heather was simply protesting her father's innocence again, Maggie said, "I know you want to protect him, but ..."

"He was in detox that night, he couldn't have been in your house."

The statement started Maggie.

"Detox?"

"Yes. It's where someone who drinks like my father drinks—"

"I know what it is."

"—goes when he has to sober up. This one's in Flemington. My father spent the night there. It's not unusual for him to go to detox for a night, then check himself out the next morning and go about his life as if nothing had happened. It's mostly just a way for him to stop drinking."

"I'm sorry."

"Not nearly as sorry as I am. Are we finished here?"

Maggie was still trying to process the information. She had no reason to disbelieve Heather, but she knew it was natural for a daughter as protective as this one to shield her father.

"You don't have to believe me," Heather said, reading Maggie's thoughts. "I'd be happy to provide you with his release papers ... if you get a warrant. Trust me, he was in detox that night and I can prove it. Now if you'll excuse me."

"Of course," Maggie said, feeling completely foolish for having come here, for having all but accused Chip McGill of breaking into her home. "Thank you for your time."

Heather offered no reply, instead giving Maggie a look of contempt. McGill did not know her, but she projected all her bitterness about her father's failed life and the people who'd ruined it onto the woman standing in front of her.

Maggie turned and headed toward the door.

"If I were you," Heather said behind her, "I'd take a closer look at the people who wanted to hurt my father. Alice Drapier was not the only one."

Maggie turned around. "Who else is there?"

"You're the amateur sleuth. When you find out, let me know. Revenge is a dish best served cold, they say. And I have some that's nearly frozen."

The comment made Maggie shiver. She suddenly wasn't sure Heather McGill was incapable of murder.

"Thank you."

"You already said that. And please don't come back."

Maggie nodded. She had caused this woman pain, and she was deeply sorry for it. But she did not regret it. Each rock she overturned led her closer to the truth. She only hoped the next one didn't hide a viper.

CHAPTER Twenty-Nine

MAGGIE HAD SPENT THE REST of the day unfocused and distracted. She'd gone to the factory after her conversation with Heather McGill, and as hard as she'd tried, she had not been able to pay attention to what was going on around her. Janice had gone over the latest accounting; Gloria and Sybil had assured her they'd completed enough stock to supply the store opening and any orders that came in for the next two weeks. Even Peter had come out of his shell, as much as was possible for a man so broken, to ask her what was wrong.

"Nothing," Maggie told him, suddenly aware how much her fixation with all things Alice was evident. *If Peter notices, it's obvious*, she'd thought, and she had tried to pull out of it.

The end of the work day came slowly but mercifully, and Maggie told them all to have a good evening as she headed home for what she hoped would be a quiet evening with her sister. Gerri had told her she had no plans for the night; her increasingly busy social calendar was free — no dinner with Tom Brightmore, no get-together with the friends Maggie knew she would make quickly in her new home. Gerri was like that: a gregarious, sometimes abrasive, firebrand who attracted friends and acquaintances easily. It would not be long, Maggie knew, before Gerri had a roster of friends to spend time with any day or evening she chose, and possibly a new manfriend. Rather than discourage Gerri, Maggie had decided to support her efforts. It could mean Gerri finding a place of her own, which would be best for both of them in Maggie's opinion. Siblings seldom made good housemates for very long.

That night they'd watched the national news and eaten pasta Gerri made. Maggie had stopped watching news several years ago, preferring to get her information online where she could choose sources she trusted.

They were enjoying cups of after dinner tea on the couch, the television muted while some sitcom played onscreen.

"So what exactly did Heather McGill tell you?" asked Gerri.

She'd been as aware as the others of Maggie's distracted state after her visit to Valley Visions.

Maggie set her cup on the coffee table. "She told me Chip could not possibly have been the intruder."

Gerri looked at her skeptically. Maggie knew she was still not convinced anyone at all had been in the house

"Maybe it was a sleepwalker," Gerri said. "You know, someone who takes a sleeping pill and ends up wandering the neighborhood. It happens. The door was open, they came in thinking it was their own home ..."

"The door was not open," Maggie bristled. "It wasn't unlocked, either. Someone was in this house. I scared them off, or the cat scared them off. It doesn't matter. What matters is that it was not Chip McGill."

"And how is Heather so sure of this?"

"Because her father was in a detox facility in Flemington."

Gerri's eyes shot up. "Really? But he was here the next morning."

"From what Heather says, that's sometimes how he stops drinking. He goes into a detox to sleep it off, then checks out in the morning."

"Sort of like a hotel."

Maggie grimaced. "I wouldn't put it that way, Gerri. The man is a serious alcoholic. Spending nights in a detox to stop drinking is not a fun stay in a Hilton somewhere."

"I didn't mean it that way."

Of course she didn't, Maggie thought. You'd have to be cold hearted to think someone like Chip McGill enjoyed his life. His daughter certainly knew better.

"What I don't understand—what has had me flummoxed all day—is why Chip would lie to me about the house key. He had two of them made. Cal Davies told me that. But why would he do that? And since he's not the one who came into the house, who was it?"

Gerri stood up and took both their empty cups.

"I suggest you sleep on it. You'll have a clear head in the morning and maybe an answer will come to you. It works for me."

As Maggie headed into the kitchen, Gerri said behind her, "I woke up one morning knowing I should move here to support you! Clear as day."

"Well, thank goodness for that," said Maggie, not quite sarcastically.

"You love having me here. Or you will, just be patient."

Maggie knew patience was in short supply. The store opening was fast approaching. Her sister was living with her in a house she'd intended to live in for years with her late husband. And a murderer was out there ... possibly the same man who had come into her house.

"Maybe he had the key made for someone else," Maggie said to herself. She was throwing out ideas now, hoping one would take hold. "Maybe he had help killing Alice, or he knows who did. Maybe I'm losing my mind ..."

She felt movement at her feet. Checks had come into the room, ready for bed. He told her what time it was by rubbing around her ankles: it was either time to eat, or time to sleep. He didn't seem to do much else.

Maggie said to him, "Yes, I know. It's time to head upstairs. I'll read awhile. That always helps me relax."

"Who are you talking to?"

Gerri was back, wiping her hands on a dish towel. Seeing Checks at Maggie's feet, she said, "Never mind."

"I'll see you in the morning."

"Going to bed so early? It's only seven o'clock."

"I'm exhausted," Maggie said. "And I'll read for an hour first. It kills the time and it's the best sleeping pill I've ever known. See you in the morning."

Maggie headed toward the stairs, with Checks padding along behind her.

She was facing several doors, too many to count. She kept trying to open them, but none budged. She felt herself growing frustrated in the dream—not frightened or panicked, but increasingly agitated when none of the doors opened.

"You're looking in the wrong direction."

It was David's voice. Maggie swiveled around, expecting to see him. He was the most frequent presence in her dreams. But he wasn't there. Just as the doors would not open, David would not reveal himself this time.

"But I'm *not*," Maggie said, in an almost pleading tone. "I'm only looking at what's in front of me. Where else would I look?"

"Behind you."

She twirled around. Nothing. Only the darkness of a dream crowded with unopened doors.

"I'm looking behind me!" she cried.

"Not there," said David's voice. "*Behind* you. Behind it all. *In the past.*"

Those three words—*in the past*—shocked her, the way a defibrillator jolts someone who's had a heart attack. The doors didn't matter. Nothing in the dream mattered. The answers she needed weren't in the dream.

She sat upright, gasping for air as if she'd swum frantically to the surface of a lake from deep within it.

Startled, Checks jumped off the bed.

Maggie sat in the dark, staring at the opposite wall, understanding two things clearly: that Alice Drapier's death was somehow connected to the murder of Lilly Stapley, and that whoever killed the girl, killed the woman ten years later.

Discovering the why of it was now her mission. It was also a dangerous one, a path that had led Alice to her death.

Maggie reached down and opened the night stand. The gun was there. She had no need of it in the dark of the night, but its presence gave her comfort, and pause. What if the person who'd come into her home hadn't been there to warn her, but to kill her?

She would pursue the answer in the morning, beginning with a look back at the disappearance of a child whose body had never been found.

"Be very careful, Maggie Dahl," she whispered to herself. "It might be behind one of those doors you dreamed about."

She eased back onto the pillow, hoping that if she closed her eyes and took ten deep breaths — or twenty, or fifty — sleep would take her again, this time without dreams.

CHAPTER Thirty

HER SISTER HAD BEEN THERE less than a week but they were quickly developing a morning routine. Maggie was ambivalent about that but admitted to herself it was comfortable. For nearly twenty-five years she'd had David to wake up to, to eat breakfast with—or not—and to share the most intimate spaces of her life. She'd been unaware (deliberately? willfully?) of the *absence* she'd felt since his death, and Gerri's arrival had brought it into stark relief. It was like living in a state of silence for six months, then suddenly finding yourself surrounded by sound. Add to that the presence of a cat, and Maggie might have to admit she liked not being alone anymore.

"A dream, you say?"

Gerri was at the table having her morning coffee. She'd toasted a bagel, smeared it with cream cheese, and set the two halves on plates for them.

Maggie finished lightening her coffee and brought it from the counter, sitting across from Gerri.

"It's weird, I know," said Maggie. "I never dreamed much until David died. I didn't remember them, anyway. But since then? Pretty much every night."

"Is he in all of them?"

"No. I'd say about half. But they're so vivid now. And this one ... there were these doors, and I kept trying to open them."

"Like on 'Let's Make a Deal.'"

"Sort of, but dangerous. I could tell by the whole

experience I wasn't going to like what I found behind any of them, but I was compelled to try. Then David said, 'Behind you,' or something like that."

"There were doors behind you?"

"I thought that's what he meant," Maggie said, "but he meant *behind* me … behind all of us, in the past."

Gerri took a bite of her bagel. She was intrigued by Maggie's story and quickly swallowed.

"Your and David's past?"

"No, that's not what he meant. He meant in Alice's past. Chip McGill's past. *Lilly Stapley's* past."

Gerri asked, "Who is Lilly Stapley?"

Maggie had kept Gerri informed of her various conversations but was not surprised she wasn't making much of an effort to remember the details.

"Lilly Stapley is the girl who disappeared ten years ago. She was twelve at the time."

"I didn't know things like that happened in Lambertville."

"They happen everywhere, Gerri. You watch all those murder shows on TV, you should know that."

It was true. Gerri was addicted to a channel that fed its viewers disappearances, death and homicide twenty-four hours a day. But having things like that happen within blocks from where you lived was still hard to imagine.

"What do you know about this Lilly Stapley thing?"

Maggie slid her plate away. She'd lost whatever appetite she had.

"Not as much as I'm going to."

Gerri watched Maggie, knowing when her sister had an idea. It was in Maggie's eyes, and the determination in her expression.

"Where are you going to find all this out?" Gerri

asked.

"From her father."

Maggie could see Gerri remembering now, realization dawning on her face.

"He works for you, doesn't he? At the factory."

"Peter Stapley. He does indeed."

"You said he was fragile, or something."

Maggie had been thinking about this all morning. She knew Peter had been nearly destroyed by his daughter's abduction. His wife had left him. They had no other children. And while it came much later than the events that ruined his life, working at Dahl House Jams had given him just a glimmer of hope, of living a few good years beyond the tragedy that defined him.

"I don't know if it's the right thing to do or not," Maggie said quietly. "But he's the only one who can tell me what really happened."

"So you think Alice's death is connected to the death of his daughter?"

"I do," said Maggie. "I think whoever killed Lilly Stapley, killed Alice Drapier. But I have no idea why. I'm hoping a careful, gentle conversation with Peter Stapley might point me in the right direction."

"Do you want me to be with you?" Gerri asked.

"No, not for this. It's going to be very delicate. He may not want to say anything, and if he doesn't, that's fine. But I have to ask. Alone with Peter, away from everyone else."

"I don't envy you, Maggie, but I trust you. And I think he will, too."

"We're going to find out." Pushing away from the table, she added, "Now if you'll excuse me, it's pill time for Checks."

They both smiled as they heard the cat flee up the

stairs. He was exceptionally smart, with a few feline superpowers, but he hated taking a pill as much as the next cat.

Maggie got up and headed to a cabinet above the sink. Taking down the pill bottle, she proceeded to stuff a small yellow tablet into a chicken-flavored Pill Pocket.

"Checks!" she called out, heading for the stairs. "Sweeties, I've got a treat for you!"

"He's not stupid," Gerri said.

Maggie ignored her, heading up after the cat. He'd feign a struggle and lightly scratch her, then surrender and take his medicine. That was the game they played.

CHAPTER Thirty-One

THE OTHERS AT THE FACTORY knew something was up when Maggie arrived. Even after David's death, during the darkest weeks of her life, she had maintained a sense of forward movement, wanting to reassure the few people who worked there that they did not need to worry about their futures. But today she was different. Today she clearly had something on her mind when she got to work.

Maggie was glad Janice was at the bank when she arrived. She had not wanted to pursue her task at hand — asking Peter Stapley to have lunch with her outside the factory — with Janice's perkiness distracting her.

"Are you okay, Mrs. Dahl?" Gloria asked.

Sybil, Gloria and Peter were preparing a small shipment to go out that afternoon.

"I'm fine," Maggie replied. Realizing her emotions were reflected on her face, she forced a smile. "I was just hoping to speak to Peter alone."

"Oh," said Sybil. "Of course. We'll go in the other room."

"That's not necessary." Turning to Peter, Maggie said, "I'd love to take you to lunch, if you can get away."

It was almost a rhetorical questions: when the boss asks if you can get away, the answer is yes. Still, Peter Stapley looked uncomfortable with the request. He'd been sealing a box when Maggie asked him. He set the roll of packing tape down and avoided looking directly at her when he replied, "Of course, I'd be happy to."

Maggie detected no enthusiasm from the man. Peter was one of those people who seemed permanently depressed. And for good reason, Maggie knew. That was what made her mission so difficult. Bringing up the subject of his dead daughter would be difficult under any circumstances—she had never done it before—and now she wanted to have a real, detailed, conversation about it.

Sybil and Gloria kept exchanging curious glances. Was Maggie going to fire him? Was she going to offer him a raise, or a better position? In such a small company, what other positions could there possibly be?

"I know just the place," said Maggie. "Don't forget your jacket."

Leaving the perplexed women behind, Maggie headed out to the car to wait while Peter got his jacket from one of the lockers David had installed for staff.

Maggie had the idea of eating at the Brightside Diner once she'd decided to go through with the lunch. There were several fine choices in town, including Bernadette's, her favorite. But she wanted to try the Brightside for the second time since moving to Lambertville, and she'd hoped Tom Brightmore might be there.

He was.

Maggie and Peter had walked over from the factory in near silence. Peter had not asked questions about why they were having lunch, and Maggie had chosen not to tell him until they were comfortably seated in a booth. Instead, they'd made small talk about the business, the weather, and the Halloween decorations in such abundance they could not be avoided this time of year.

"Did you ever go in for the full Halloween treatment?" Maggie asked at one point as they strolled up Union Street.

She immediately regretted it. She knew Peter no longer lived in the house he'd occupied with his wife and daughter. His wife was long gone, no doubt unable to keep living in a town that held only unbearable memories for her; and his daughter had been taken in a moment, somehow abducted in broad daylight a decade ago. If the Stapleys had indulged in the Halloween festivities so beloved by the town, it would have been when they were all alive and happy.

"No," Peter replied, staring straight ahead. "Not since …"

He left the sentence unfinished.

"I understand, and I apologize for asking. I wasn't thinking."

"No need to apologize, Mrs. Dahl. I never expected anyone to live with what I do. It's easy for other people to forget. I imagine you know how that feels."

Maggie caught his sideways glance at her. He was right. It had only been six months since David's death, but everyone else had moved on. Everyone except Maggie and their son Wynn, and even he had recovered remarkably well. He was young, with his entire life ahead of him. There was no reason for him not to get on with it.

They crossed Bridge Street, turned right and reached the Brightside Diner two blocks later having said nothing more.

Maggie had only been to the diner one other time.

She held the door for Peter as they entered. It wasn't crowded—none of the restaurants had an especially busy weekday service—plus it was mid-day, not breakfast, not lunch, and not the kind of place that did much brunch business. There were, by Maggie's quick count, only seven other people in the restaurant, including a server, cook, and the owner himself.

Tom Brightmore was taller than Maggie remembered him, passing the six feet mark by several inches. He was dressed casually in a flannel shirt and jeans, and he hurried over to welcome them as they entered.

"Morning, folks," he said, indicating he did not immediately recognize Maggie. "Sit anywhere you'd like."

Maggie chose a booth by the window. It allowed them to see outside, and it was well away from the few other customers. She wanted as much privacy as they could get.

Tom held out menus to them once they'd seated themselves.

Maggie looked up and was struck by the blueness of his eyes, eyes that matched his smile. Maggie had always noticed when someone's expression was not reflected in their eyes; it was a good, quick way to detect insincerity. Tom Brightmore struck her as very sincere, as well as gentle, well-mannered and immediately likable.

"Judy will be over to take your orders," he said. "In the meantime, can I get you some coffee?"

Maggie and Peter both said yes, then Maggie added, "My sister Gerri says hello."

That stopped him. "Oh, you're Maggie Dahl! Of course. I'm so sorry. I know you, I met your late husband once, and I've just had the pleasure of meeting your sister Gerri."

Maggie wanted to say it was good someone found it a pleasure, but she held her tongue.

"I'll get your coffee. If you need anything, Judy will take care of you, or just wave. I'll be behind the counter."

He walked off, leaving Maggie with a good impression of the man who might be dating her sister if things progressed. She could have thought about it more, or even engaged Brightmore in conversation, but she was not here about her sister's social life. She was here about the murder of a twelve-year-old girl named Lilly Stapley, whose father was sitting across from her.

"What did you want to talk about, Mrs. Dahl?" Peter said.

It occurred to Maggie that he really had no idea why they'd come here.

"Your daughter," she said, choosing to be direct. "I think what happened to her is connected to my neighbor's death, and possibly more."

Peter said nothing, extending his silence to the point of discomfort, while Tom Brightmore brought their coffee over. Sensing something intimate between them, he set the cups down, said, "Enjoy," and left them alone.

Taking a deep breath, Peter Stapley began recounting for Maggie what happened one beautiful, perfect day in October. A day much like the one they saw outside the diner window. A day when nothing could go wrong, and everything did.

CHAPTER Thirty-Two

THE COUNTRY WAS A MONTH away from electing Barack Obama to the presidency. There was a feeling of renewal in the air, even from many who had no intention of voting for him. After eight years of war and an administration much of the American public had soured on, the prospect of a young, vibrant, gifted politician bringing something new to America was exciting. You could feel it in the air. You could hear it on the airwaves and read about it on this relatively new thing called the Internet. And you could see it in the yard signs posted around Lambertville, where many people were quite happy with the idea of a President Obama.

Peter and Melissa Stapley were not among those especially thrilled with the prospect. Both lifelong Republicans, they were unenthused about a McCain-Palin ticket, but they planned on voting for them anyway. Neither had ever been politically active beyond their circle of friends, most of whom were caught up in the excitement of electing a Democrat. Government policy just wasn't important to the Stapleys. They weren't uncomfortable living in a liberal enclave like Lambertville, but they kept their opinions to themselves and often wished more people would do the same.

It was a bright, sunny, October day. Melissa, Peter and their daughter, Lilly, had gone to Bernadette's for breakfast, a favorite restaurant they treated themselves to every Saturday. The Stapley family sitting in a window booth was a familiar sight to other diners there, as well as to passersby on the street. They often waited just to get that table. Lilly, twelve

198

years old as of August, loved watching people she knew walk by, and making comments to her parents about strangers, most of whom she knew were tourists. Lambertville was a destination, particularly on cool, clear, sunny days like this. They might come from ten miles away, or fifty, but they came and they strolled and they smiled as they explored a small river town with so much to offer.

At twelve, Lilly was very capable of being on her own. They lived a mere four blocks away, and Lilly was known around town for her friendliness. She was often seen talking to shopkeepers and neighbors. And while some might think she should not be alone — or be as outgoing as she was, sometimes with people she'd just met — twelve was not an unreasonable age to go around by oneself.

They'd just finished breakfast. Ruth, an older waitress who worked at Bernadette's and had been a friend of the restaurant's namesake before her passing, was clearing their table when there was a tap at the window. The Stapleys had not been paying attention to the outside when the tap came, and they all turned suddenly at the sound. Standing outside, his face inches from the glass, was Chip McGill.

Melissa forced herself to smile, while Peter gave a genuine wave and Lilly said loudly, "Hello, Mr. McGill!" flapping her hand at him.

"I don't like that man," Melissa said through her strained smile, as if she were a ventriloquist keeping her lips from moving.

"He's harmless," said Peter, watching as Lilly leaned forward toward the window.

"He's drunk."

"We don't know that."

"Well, I don't like him and I don't have to."

Peter shot her a look: not in front of Lilly, please. He did not want his daughter's opinion of the handyman poisoned by

199

her mother's dislike of him.

Chip waved a last time and headed up the street toward the bridge. Ruth returned with the check, and Peter quickly put two ten dollar bills on the table and rose. It was time to leave.

Melissa wanted to stop at the jewelers to pick up a watch she'd had repaired. Peter wanted to buy a pound of custom coffee from the coffee shop three doors down. Lilly wanted neither.

"I'll just stay here," Lilly said, plopping down on the bench outside Bernadette's.

"Are you sure?" Melissa asked. "You'll get bored here."

"People never bore me," Lilly replied. She had a vivid imagination, and enjoyed making up lives for strangers she saw walking down the street. She even wrote stories about them, and declared that she wanted to be a writer when she grew up so she could take readers on the fabulous adventures in her mind.

"It's a nice day," Peter said in his daughter's defense. "Let her stay here."

Melissa wasn't comfortable with it for some reason. It was as if the sight of Chip McGill staring into the window at them had given her a premonition. Still, she'd let Lilly wander alone many times and no harm had come of it. Her daughter was a very smart child, capable and mature for her age. She nodded reluctantly and headed to the jewelry store.

"I'll be back in five minutes," Peter said to Lilly. "Don't go far."

It was the last thing he ever said to his daughter. He returned to an empty bench. An empty sidewalk. An empty street. And, soon, an empty life. Not only had his child gone far, she had gone so far he would never see her again.

By sundown the search was a town affair. Melissa Stapley had not yet turned her fury on her husband. After all, she had agreed to let Lilly stay behind on the bench. But within a surprisingly short time she blamed Peter for all of it. He was the one who'd convinced her to ignore her instinct and leave Lilly alone that day. He was the one who assured her nothing could go wrong. He was the one who told her the alcoholic handyman staring at them through the restaurant window was harmless. He was the one she had to leave, along with Lambertville itself, a year after Lilly was gone and presumed dead. For what else would someone do with a twelve-year-old girl, once he'd sexually assaulted her? What good would she be? Of course she was dead. She was not coming home. Peter could stay in this godforsaken town and wait until his last stinking breath. She would not, and did not.

Flyers stayed up for almost two years. Every few months a story ran in the local media, just to remind people that a girl had vanished on a clear, beautiful October day.

A young police officer named Bryan Hoyt, first on the scene when the Stapleys called the police, progressed through the small ranks of a small town police department to become a sergeant.

Peter Stapley lost his wife. Lost his house. Lost his job. And didn't care.

That day had been the beginning of an end he was still waiting for and that he told Maggie Dahl about while they ate at the Brightside Diner, ten years later and a world away.

CHAPTER Thirty-Three

MAGGIE SAT IN STUNNED SILENCE. She had been uncertain if talking to Peter was the right thing to do, and now she was even more unsure. The man sitting across from her in a booth at the Brightside Diner was still broken. She hadn't fully realized that until this morning. She'd known Peter had been "getting back on his feet" for years, and she'd hoped working at Dahl House Jams was a major step in his painstakingly slow recovery. But now she couldn't say. He seemed depleted by telling her what happened, as if recalling it all had peeled open a wound that, by its nature, could never heal.

"I'm sorry," Maggie said, forcing herself not to avoid his gaze.

"Don't be, Mrs. Dahl. I hadn't thought about it a while, not in detail, anyway."

Great, Maggie thought. *I encouraged this man to relive the central horror of his life over eggs and toast. Good going, Mrs. Dahl.*

They'd come this far, so Maggie carefully took another step, asking, "Did you ever think it was someone from town who took Lilly?"

"I never doubted it," Peter replied without hesitation.

Maggie was surprised at his certainty.

"Was there anyone in particular?"

Peter looked at her quizzically. He was a smart man and he could tell Maggie had someone in mind. She was fishing for an answer she already had.

Sliding his half-eaten breakfast away, Peter said, "Well, I know who it wasn't."

Maggie was surprised by the statement. She leaned up, waiting for him to continue. She saw a slight smile cross his lips, as if, despite the pain of remembering what had happened to his child, he was enjoying making Maggie wait. *Good*, she thought. *Let him take enjoyment where he can.*

"It wasn't Chip McGill," Peter said at last. "That I can tell you."

"How do you know it—"

"I heard the rumors," he continued, cutting her off. "I know where they started, too, with Alice Drapier. I never knew why she was so sure it was him, and I didn't care. I just knew it wasn't."

"But he was there that day," Maggie said. "Leering in the window at your family."

Peter turned serious, almost hard. "He wasn't 'leering' at us—not at me, not at Melissa, not at Lilly. He's a good man. I grew up with him. If there is anything I know, it's that Chip did not harm my child."

"Did the police question him?"

"Of course they did! They questioned everyone. After he saw us at the restaurant he went straight to work on Jared Leightner's guest house. He was fixing it up for the old man to rent. The police checked the time. They spoke to Jared. There was no way Chip could have had time to do anything to Lilly, even if he'd wanted to. And he didn't! What Alice did to him was evil and destructive."

It was a lot to digest. It was also time to go back to work. Peter's mood had soured more from talking about Chip and Alice than it had telling her about the day Lilly disappeared. Maggie waved at Judy for the check.

A moment later they left the diner. Tom Brightmore was busy with a customer and didn't see them leave. Maggie knew they would have another chance to talk, and after their brief encounter she felt better about it. She would caution her sister not to rush into anything, but she would not discourage it.

Outside, they began walking toward the corner when Maggie looked across the street and saw Sergeant Hoyt coming out of the bank. He was dressed in civilian clothes and Maggie assumed it was his day off.

"Peter," Maggie said, "I need to talk to someone. Do you mind meeting me back at the factory?"

"Not at all, Mrs. Dahl. I can use the walk to think. Especially after talking about all that."

The light changed and Peter headed up Union.

Not wanting to miss her chance, Maggie jaywalked, waving at Hoyt, who was about to get into his car. "Sergeant!" she shouted. "Excuse me! Sergeant Hoyt!"

Maggie could tell Hoyt was not happy having his morning disturbed. When he saw her, he closed his car door and stood next to it in the street. He crossed his arms over his chest.

"What now?"

"I'm sorry to bother you, Sergeant—"

"No, you're not."

Undeterred, Maggie continued, "I just had breakfast with Peter Stapley."

"I saw that," said Hoyt, looking down the street as Peter walked off in the distance.

"Anyway, we talked about Lilly, his daughter, and

he told me he was certain Chip McGill had nothing to do with it."

Hoyt sighed: here we go again.

"And this is significant because …?"

"Because Chip had two keys to my house made, with two receipts. He wanted a key my husband didn't know about."

"I'd say you're confusing me, but you've been doing that since we met. What does Chip having a key to your house have to do with Lilly Stapley?"

"I don't know," Maggie said, exasperated. "But I believe it does. I believe it's all connected — Alice's murder, Lilly's abduction, the intruder in my house."

Hoyt waited a moment, either calming himself or thinking what to ask next, Maggie wasn't sure.

"How do you know about the second key?" he asked, honestly curious now.

"Because Cal Davies told me."

"Cal Davies?"

"Yes!" said Maggie. "He told me Chip had two keys made, not one, and he asked for two receipts. So he could give David a key and receipt back, saying he didn't want it. But he kept one, you see? Maybe he keeps keys to other people's houses, maybe he's been doing this for years."

Maggie waited for Hoyt to respond while he thought about what she'd said.

"Sergeant Hoyt?" she prompted.

Hoyt had humored her as long as he could. "I don't want to be rude," he said. "But I really don't have time for your speculation. My wife's waiting at home."

"Your wife?"

"Yes, I have a life you don't know about, and I plan to keep it that way."

He opened his car door and got in.

"But will you think about it?" Maggie asked hurriedly.

"About *what?*" he asked, not hiding his irritation.

"About Chip. The keys. All of it."

"I haven't stopped thinking about it," Hoyt replied, taking a deep breath as he reached for his seat belt and closed the door.

Maggie realized they'd been standing in the street. She hurried around the back of the car to the sidewalk and watched as Hoyt drove away.

CHAPTER Thirty-Four

MAGGIE WAS TRYING TO MAKE sense of it all, to *decipher* the clues she'd found the past few days. Instead of going back to the factory where she'd be distracted by people and responsibilities, she headed home after calling Janice to let her know her change in plans. It was just as well. Chip was coming in an hour to start another project, retiling the bathrooms, beginning with the one Gerri was using. It meant the sisters would have to share a bathroom for a few days, a prospect Maggie dreaded, but one she would deal with, as she was dealing with everything about her new housemate.

She arrived home to find Chip sitting on the porch eating his lunch from a paper bag, his toolbox on the step next to him.

Maggie parked in the driveway and walked up to him.

"You're early, Chip," she said, as he stood up to greet her.

"I'd shake your hand but I got some chicken salad on my fingers," Chip said.

"I think we passed the handshaking stage a few months ago," Maggie replied, forcing a smile. "Come on in."

He rolled up his lunch bag, grabbed his toolbox and followed her to the door. As she led them into the house, he said, "Mr. Collier had to reschedule some work I'm doing on his office so I took the liberty of having my lunch on your porch. Hope you don't mind."

"Not at all. The timing's perfect, actually," Maggie replied as they entered the living room. "I just had lunch with Peter Stapley and came back here instead of the factory."

She saw a pained look on Chip's face at the mention of Stapley.

"How is Peter doing?" Chip asked, using Stapley's first name in a rare show of familiarity. "I know it's coming up on ten years since that whole kidnapping business. Everybody in town knows."

"It's tragic. I didn't realize just how big it was ... I mean, the murder of a child is as big as it gets, but the Lilly Stapley kidnapping touched so many lives here."

"Yes, it did."

Maggie saw an opportunity and took it, not wasting time debating with herself about the propriety of it.

"Yours, too, from what I know," Maggie said.

Chip stared at her, unsure where she was going with it.

"I know you saw the Stapleys the day Lilly went missing."

His expression went from pained to hard. "I had nothing to do with it."

"I believe that, Chip," Maggie said. "Peter said as much."

"He's a good man."

"You both are, but I have to ask you about something."

Visibly steeling himself, Chip asked, "What would that be?"

"Someone came into this house a few nights ago. That's why I asked you about the key my husband had you make for yourself."

"I gave it back to him, Mrs. Dahl. I told you that."

"I know you did, Chip."

She sighed. She'd gone this far and decided to spell it all out.

"I asked Cal Davies about it, on the off chance he remembered making the key, and he said yes. In fact, he said, you made two keys ..."

"Why would he say that?" Chip nearly shouted. "That's not true!"

"Let's assume it's not, then. Why would Cal Davies lie about having keys made to my house?"

"Why would Alice tell people I was the one who took Lilly Stapley?" Chip said angrily. "Why do people say evil things about other people? I don't know, but I didn't have two keys made, and the one I brought back, I gave to Mr. Dahl."

It hit Maggie then, with the force of a blow. She knew in that instant it was not Chip who had lied, or Chip who had come into her home with a key he'd had made. *It was the man who made keys himself.* Who knew how many he'd duplicated, or why? How many houses he entered when no one was home, or why.

"I believe you," Maggie said quietly. "I know now you're not the one who was lying."

Her words took a moment to sink in. They'd been standing in the living room having a conversation about false accusations, home intrusions and murder, when the import of Maggie's confession hit home. Chip walked to the arm chair and sat down, dazed by what he'd learned.

"It was Cal Davies," Chip said, his voice almost a whisper.

Maggie sat on the couch across from him.

Chip slowly looked up at her. "It was all Cal Davies.

Lilly Stapley. Alice Drapier. Your visitor here."

"I wouldn't call an intruder a visitor, but yes, that's where this seems to be heading."

"You should tell the police."

"I did, sort of," said Maggie. "I ran into Sergeant Hoyt after lunch."

"Did you tell him about Cal?"

"Only that Cal had implicated you."

Chip sat breathing and thinking for several moments as the implications set in.

"He ruined my life. He ruined my marriage. He destroyed my family. He killed a child, and probably Alice. He can't get away with this."

His tone sent a chill through Maggie. Had she told him things he would be better off not knowing? Had she opened their own Pandora's box right here in Lambertville?

"He won't get away with it," she said. "But there has to be evidence."

"Alice has been dead almost a week and there's been nothing."

Maggie watched his face soften and realized that despite what Alice had done to him, Chip still felt something for her, even if it was just compassion for a sad and brutal death.

"We don't know what Hoyt and the police have, or where they're at with their investigation. Let them do what they're trained for."

"Sure," he said bitterly. "Like they solved Lilly Stapley's murder. That girl vanished ten years ago and they never found her body, never found a single shred of evidence. I don't trust them to do much better now."

Maggie got up from the couch. "We have to," she said, even as her mind began to formulate a next step.

"Remember, Chip, killers kill, that's what they do. Alice found that out the hard way. We don't want anyone else being harmed."

"No," he said, sending another cold wave through her, "we don't." Rising from the chair, he added, "I think it's time for me to get to work."

Maggie nodded and watched as Chip headed upstairs to the second bathroom.

She kept hearing one word in her head: *evidence.* If she only had evidence of Cal Davies's involvement with any of it. If the police just had proof …

Was there a way for her to find it? Did she dare even look?

Yes, Maggie, she told herself. *In fact, you have no other choice.*

She would have to act, to flush out her prey … for she had to admit she was now a predator. The vital question, the one of life and death, was which of them would prove to be more dangerous.

CHAPTER Thirty-Five

"WHAT MOVIE ARE YOU GOING to see?" Maggie asked.

She'd been watching her sister become giddy over the course of the evening, waiting for Tom to pick her up for dinner and a movie in Doylestown, Pennsylvania, a thirty minute drive from the house. Giddy was not Gerri's style.

"It's some kind of comedy we thought we'd both like," Gerri replied, fussing for the tenth time with her sweater.

"Some kind of comedy?" Maggie repeated. "How do you know you'll like it if you don't even know the title?"

They were in the kitchen. Maggie had made herself a sandwich of sliced turkey and Swiss cheese, unsure if she even wanted that much to eat. The day had left her stomach in knots.

Gerri cocked one hand on her hip and leaned against the counter with the other.

"I'll like it because I'm with Tom," she said. "Why are you so worried? He likes you."

Maggie was surprised to know Tom had said anything about her, considering how brief their conversation had been at lunch.

"Yes," Gerri continued. "I know you spoke to him at the diner today."

"Barely."

"And I know you were there with Peter Stapley."

Maggie knew Peter was a fixture in town, as well as in the town's imagination. Of course Tom would know who he was.

"What was that about?" Gerri asked.

"I wanted to talk to him about his daughter's disappearance."

"That must have made for light conversation."

Getting to the point, Maggie said, "It wasn't Chip."

Gerri took her hand off the counter, straightening up.

"What do you mean?"

"Chip had nothing to do with Lilly Stapley's abduction and murder. He had nothing to do with breaking into this house, and he did not lie to me about having a secret key made so he could do god-knows-what in the middle of the night while we slept."

"You learned all this from lunch with Peter?"

Maggie put the uneaten half of her sandwich down. She was not going to finish it.

"No, Gerri. I learned that Peter never suspected Chip and has considered him innocent all this time. However, I do think—I *believe*—it was Cal Davies who lied to me about the keys."

"Which means he's part of it all."

"Yes."

"Including Alice's murder?"

"Up to and including Alice's murder. If he had anything to do with what happened to Lilly Stapley, who knows what else he's done? But Cal is the answer to all these questions."

A car horn sounded outside. Maggie glanced toward the front door, forming a sudden, unfavorable, impression of Tom Brightmore.

"He's not coming to the door?"

"Don't be so quick to judge," Gerri said, grabbing her purse off the kitchen counter. "I told him to honk the horn when he got here. Stop looking for reasons to dislike him. And stop thinking I'm not a big girl who can take care of myself. There will not be a husband number four."

Gerri quickly kissed Maggie on the cheek and hurried out of the kitchen, saying behind her, "I want to hear more about this. And I want you to contact Sergeant Hoyt."

Maggie followed along to the front door.

"I already did, and I think I planted a seed. He took me seriously about Cal Davies. At least I think he did."

"So let him take it from there."

Gerri opened the door. They could see a brown Ford Focus parked against the curb. The passenger window slid down and Tom leaned over, waving at the women on the porch.

"Hello, Maggie!" he called. "She told me to honk!"

Ah, thought Maggie, *he knows it's not so gentlemanly to wait on the street.* And *he cares what I think.*

Maggie waved back, then said to Gerri, "Maybe I'll

wait for the police on this. Maybe not. I'm *this* close ..."

"To getting killed, just like Alice. Don't do anything stupid. Or more stupid than you've already done."

Gerri hurried down the steps.

Calling after her, Maggie, said, "You're the one who wanted to go into her house!"

Gerri waved behind her, not responding. She got into Tom's car and shut the door.

Maggie stood on the porch, watching them drive up the street.

Don't do anything stupid.

The words weren't unfamiliar to her. She'd heard them many times in her life: from her parents when she'd first met David and told them he was the man she'd spend her life with; from her friends when she'd told them they were moving to Lambertville; almost every time she'd done something daring, something others might not have the courage to do.

Like dating a man ten years younger in a town you just moved to ...

She smiled at the thought. She was cautioning her sister not to do anything stupid with a man she just met. If Maggie was going to take risks, she had to allow others to do the same.

And with that thought she knew what she had to do

DAY 6

"Did St. Francis preach to the birds? Whatever for?
If he really liked birds, he would have done better to
preach to the cats."

– Rebecca West

CHAPTER Thirty-Six

MAGGIE WOKE UP WITH A sense of foreboding. She had never been given to premonitions, including the night David died—the one time in her life when she wished the universe had sent her a warning. But this morning she sensed something was going to happen. She could not discern if that something was good or bad, only that it was important and would change the course of her life, if not the lives of others.

Gerri was awake when Maggie headed down for her morning coffee. She'd expected her sister to sleep in, regardless of what time she'd come home from her night out with Tom Brightmore. But there Gerri was, sitting at the kitchen table reading a copy of the New York Times with a cup of coffee in front of her and a single, dry piece of whole wheat toast on a paper plate. She was wearing the flowing floral housecoat she'd brought with her, draped over cotton pajamas.

"Up so early?" Maggie asked, walking to the counter and taking a cup down from the cabinet.

"I wasn't home that late," Gerri replied.

Maggie poured herself coffee, wondering if something had gone wrong.

"Everything okay? With your evening, I mean."

"Oh, yes," Gerri replied cheerfully. "Everything is great. Tom is a good man, Maggie. Younger than me, but we don't need to keep pointing that out, do we?"

"No," said Maggie. "We're no spring chickens, so being a decade younger than you still puts him at, what, thirty-nine?"

"Forty in December."

"So you know his birthday. Did you put it in your calendar?" Maggie teased.

"As a matter of fact, I did." Gerri took a bite of toast, then asked, "Do you ever miss it?"

"Do I miss what?"

"New York!" Gerri pointed at the newspaper. "The greatest city in the world."

"I'm sure they say the same thing in Paris, London, Chicago … Philadelphia. Speaking of which, why are you reading the New York Times, and where did you get it?"

"It's yesterday's," Gerri said. "Tom had it in his car and gave it to me. I know Philly's closer, but it's still *The New York Times*."

Maggie took a seat across from her. "In answer to your question, yes and no. I miss my friends, I miss some of the things the city has to offer, but the stress? The almost mindless frenetic pace? Not at all. I'd had enough. We both had."

"Then you made the right move, and you found the right place."

"I believe we did," Maggie said.

Gerri slid the paper aside. "What's your next move, Inspector Dahl? I know you have one. We didn't have time to talk about much last night, but I can see the wheels turning."

"You always could," Maggie replied. "I think it's time to visit Cal Davies again."

"What for, Maggie? I thought you were going to leave this to the police."

"I am … for the most part. But I think rattling his cage might speed things up, shake something loose."

"Like a murder weapon? They already have that."

"More like a mistake," Maggie said. "Get him nervous. Nervous people sometimes do stupid things."

"And sometimes they don't. What if all you accomplish is letting him know *you* know he lied to you? And isn't that really all you know at this point? You can't prove he was the intruder. You can't prove he killed Alice, or that he had anything at all to do with kidnapping that child."

"I had a sense when I woke up this morning," Maggie said. "Call it prescience, or just this unexpected certainty. He is at the center of it, Gerri. And I'm going to put him on notice, that's all. Get him sweating a little while Sergeant Hoyt takes the information I gave him and runs with it."

"But you don't know that he is."

"And I don't know that he's not."

Gerri stood up from the table. "I don't like it, Maggie, not at all. What do you think, Checks?"

Maggie looked down and saw the cat sitting on its haunches between them. She'd not heard or seen him come in and she reminded herself to get used to having a living, breathing, phantom in the house. A shadow that meowed.

Checks expressed no opinion but kept staring up at Gerri's empty plate.

"He wants food," said Gerri.

"He always wants food."

Maggie got up and walked to the pantry where she kept the cat food, a new staple in the house. Gerri headed out of the kitchen, saying as she left, "I'd tell you not to do anything foolish, but I'd be wasting my breath."

"Let's make a deal," Maggie called after her. "I

won't warn you off Tom Brightmore and you won't warn me off finding Alice's killer."

Gerri did not respond, heading quickly up the stairs.

Looking at Checks, who had strolled up beside her, Maggie said, "So was that a yes or a no? She didn't say."

The cat cried. He didn't care about deals, dates or murder. He wanted food.

She took out a can of chicken paté, thinking it was a ridiculous thing to call cat food, and reached for a clean bowl. Checks would have his breakfast, Gerri would have her romantic life, and Maggie would have her killer.

CHAPTER Thirty-Seven

MAGGIE WASN'T SURE WHAT HER plan was or if she had any. She only knew she needed to visit Davies Hardware again, steel herself for any eventuality, and get to it.

She'd left her car at home and walked into town. After her visit, she would pick up the car and head to the factory. Everything was in place now, and the store opening was only two nights away. Fretting had never been in her nature, not even when they'd moved to Lambertville — easily the most stress-inducing thing she'd done since they'd been married, aside from having a child — but now it was part of her everyday experience. Stress over the business, stress over the store, stress over her sister, and, though she only admitted it to herself, stress over a life without her rock, without David. Whether it was true or not, she believed David would know exactly what to do in the circumstances in which she found herself. He would know how to confront a man she was certain had invaded her home. He would even know how to corner a killer, leaving the capture to those with experience and authority.

She wondered if Sergeant Hoyt had done anything with the information she'd given him about Davies, or if he'd even considered it *information*, as opposed to speculation and possibly paranoia. She would not disturb him again, and suspected he would not let her. The time had come to do what little she could by herself and see what came of it, as long as it was not a hammer to her own skull.

Cal was alone at the cash register when Maggie walked in. It was only her second time in the store and she was wondering if he had any employees when, looking at a list in his hand, he called out to someone in the back of the store, "Joey, we need two gallons of semi-gloss white for Mrs. Geller's order. Her son's coming by in an hour to pick it up. You got that?"

A man's voice called back, "On it, Cal."

Maggie couldn't see the man in back but judged him from his voice to be young.

Looking up from his list, he saw Maggie and said, "Morning, Mrs. Dahl. Back so soon?"

"The house is a lot of work," Maggie said. "Chip always needs something or other."

Maggie watched Davies's expression for any change, any hint of wariness at the mention of Chip, but saw none. If she'd thought it would strike a nerve with him, she'd been wrong.

"That's the nature of the handyman business," he said. "If it's not one thing, it's another. Anything I can help you with?"

"No, I think I can find my way around."

Maggie headed into the aisles acting as if she didn't know what she was looking for but would find it on her own.

She heard a machine of some kind whir to life. Reaching the end of an aisle, she saw what it was: a paint mixer on a narrow table, shaking a can of what she assumed was semi-gloss white for Mrs. Geller, whoever that was. Standing next to it was the young man who'd called out a minute earlier.

"Hello," Maggie said.

"Morning," came the reply. He was not paying attention to her, instead looking at his smartphone, cupped in his hand and held by his side to better hide it from his boss.

Maggie recognized him from town but didn't know his name. Given his lack of interest in human interaction at the moment, she turned and headed back up another aisle, seeing midway along it what she was looking for.

Back at the cash register, Maggie placed the hammer on the counter.

Davies did not miss a beat.

"Is that all for you today?"

Maggie stared at him; he returned the stare with a smile.

"You know," Maggie said, "this hammer looks exactly like the one I found next to Alice Drapier's body. I'm sure you've heard I'm the one who discovered her. The whole town knows by now."

Ringing up the hammer, he said, "I don't really engage in gossip. But yes, I'd heard something about that."

"Maybe the person who killed poor Alice bought the hammer here."

And maybe that person was you, she thought.

"It's possible, Mrs. Dahl. I'm the only hardware store in Lambertville. But there's always True Value in New Hope. And considering there are probably a thousand hammers exactly like this one floating around the county, it's just as likely they got it somewhere else."

Maggie felt doubt creeping in as she handed him her credit card.

"I think you were mistaken about the keys," she

said.

Ignoring her, he replied, "Do you need a bag for this?"

"No, thank you. I just want to let you know I don't think Chip had two keys made."

"I may have been mistaken," he said. "Chip's had a lot of keys made over the years. Or maybe it was someone else. I apologize if I accidentally misinformed you. I could go back and check my receipts if you know what day it was."

Maggie's uncertainty was now pronounced. "It's perfectly all right. Mistakes happen. I just wanted to clear that up."

"And buy a hammer that looks familiar," he said, sliding the claw hammer toward her.

She stared down at it, at his hand, his fingers so close to the grip.

"Yes, thank you."

She picked up the hammer and took the receipt from him.

"I hope to see you at the store opening," she said.

"I wouldn't miss it for the world."

The words stopped her for just a beat, something in the way he'd said them. No longer trusting her own instincts, worried they'd been clouded by her imagination, she took the hammer and left the store.

She did not hear Cal Davies through the store window calling out for Joey. She did not hear him tell his young employee that he needed to leave for a while, that he had something to do. And she did not see him watch her walk away, wait several moments after she'd crossed the street, then leave the store himself.

Something told her to look back, but by the time she turned around as casually as she could, there was no one there.

CHAPTER Thirty-Eight

"I DON'T LIKE IT," GERRI said.

Maggie had returned home after her trip to Davies Hardware, rattled but still convinced Davies was at the center of it all. She didn't want her obsession with finding Alice's killer to affect those around her more than it already had, with the exception of her sister.

They were standing in the kitchen, with Maggie pacing back and forth while she sorted it all out in her mind.

"It's just a look-see," Maggie explained. "A harmless stroll—"

"Around someone's private property!"

"He won't be there. He's at work."

Gerri had grown increasingly alarmed as Maggie told her about her plan to visit Cal Davies's house while he worked. She'd expressed her concern and cautioned Maggie to stop before it was too late.

"Maybe he has a dog," Gerri said, trying to dissuade her. "Or one of those motion alarms that goes off if you snoop around the yard."

"I don't know that I would call it snooping"

"Well for godsake, what else would you call it, Maggie? This has gone far enough. Too far, for my taste."

"Tell that to Alice. Tell that to Lilly Stapley."

Gerri sighed, exasperated. "You don't know that he had anything to do with the girl's disappearance, or your neighbor's murder. But if he did, you've tipped your hand now, haven't you?"

Maggie stopped at the sink, her back to the window overlooking the yard. A week ago she might have seen Alice wandering around — a sight no one would ever see again.

"That was the point, Gerri, to let him know someone was onto him."

"And what if you're wrong? What if your imagination has run so wild it's got you into a corner of your own making? Let's say he's innocent, Maggie, that he's only a killer in your fantasies, then what? Think about the harm done to Chip McGill over that kind of speculation."

Maggie's face fell. She had not taken that possibility into account. She'd assumed she was correct, believed she had to be. And even if she was wrong, or partially wrong (perhaps Cal Davies had killed Alice but had nothing to do with the child), she was not spreading rumors about him.

"My mind is made up," Maggie said. "I'm just going to take a look around. I'll take something with me, a gift of some kind ..."

Maggie quickly searched the kitchen cupboards. She found an unopened jar of peach jam, one of their first efforts, with an early version of the Dahl House Jams logo on it.

"It's a prop," explained Maggie. "Really for anyone who might see me — they'll think I'm taking something to everyone's favorite hardware store owner. And if someone answers the door, well, I just thought Cal might like to try some of our product."

"It's too dangerous," Gerri said. "I'm going with you."

Holding up her hand, Maggie said, "No, no, no.

He's not home, I'm telling you. He's at work, I was just there. He lives alone. I'm going to ring the doorbell, and when he doesn't answer, I'll take a quick walk around the property."

Just like Alice did.

The thought had been nagging at her ever since she'd concluded Cal Davies was a liar and probable killer. Alice had wandered into Maggie's living room. Alice had wandered many places she was not welcomed or expected. It's one of the things Alice did. And, Maggie now believed, it's what likely got her killed. But where had she wandered? Whose home was the last she'd clumsily invaded?

"I don't like it."

"You don't have to," Maggie said, reaching for her purse.

"Take the gun."

Gerri blurted it out. She'd never even seen a gun up close until Maggie had come downstairs with David's in her hand.

"I don't know about that," Maggie replied, hesitating. It had not occurred to her to take the precaution of being armed.

"It fits in your purse, doesn't it?"

"Of course. It's not a shotgun."

"Then take it," Gerri urged. "Since you won't take me. I'm serious, Maggie."

Thinking it through and deciding it couldn't hurt—the gun would be in her purse, nowhere else—Maggie relented.

"Fine. I'll just look at it as taking a part of David with me. He was always good luck for me."

Until he died in his sleep and you woke up next to a dead husband.

Giving in to the suggestion she take the firearm with her, she hurried upstairs for the gun.

Coming back downstairs, her sister out of sight, Maggie left the house with a jar of jam in one hand and a purse slung over her arm that concealed a Glock. Anyone seeing her walking down the sidewalk would have no idea what they were really looking at.

Maggie felt a strange calmness come over her, as if knowing everything had been set in motion and all she had to do now was prepare for an outcome she could not foretell.

CHAPTER Thirty-Nine

MAGGIE HAD PASSED CAL DAVIES'S house many times but had never known it was his. He lived on Clinton Street, just two and a half blocks from Maggie's home. She and David had taken daily walks, rescheduled to evening walks after they started the business, and she'd seen the unassuming two-story home the way she'd seen many homes along her their route—as houses dotting a neighborhood like hundreds of others. Only the very large homes drew her attention, or ones with elaborate gardens or statements of some kind. (Just as the residents indulged in Halloween with great flare, many made their political views known with yard signs and porch decorations.)

Davies's house was in the middle of the block. It had been easy to find out which one he lived in with just a few minutes of online searching. The house was white with yellow trim, a modest front porch, a tall hedge in front, and a wooden fence encircling the property.

Maggie stood on the sidewalk looking at the front window. There was no sign of activity inside. She had no idea what she would do if someone answered the door, but she needed to be certain she could quickly explore the outside of the house without raising suspicion from the neighbors. She took a deep breath, walked up onto the porch and rang the doorbell. No answer. Thirty seconds later, she rang again.

Reassured there was no one home, she decided to

be bold and peer into the picture window to the left of the door. "Yoo-hoo!" she called out, pretending to still try and get an occupant's attention. "Anybody home!"

The window looked onto a living room notable only for its blandness. It appeared Cal Davies had no affection for knick-knacks, photographs or books. There was a beige couch, a single book case with just a few volumes accented by several porcelain statues, the kind you'd find in a gift card shop. A passive television was mounted on one wall. Other than the obligatory recliner and a coffee table, that was it. She could see a hallway leading back into the house, a staircase case leading up, and what she assumed was a closet door.

Stepping back from the window, Maggie glanced around the house. She tried to think like Alice. If Alice had come here and found herself in a deadly situation, what had she seen, and where had she gone?

Keeping a smile on her face, Maggie glanced up and around, looking out at the street, across it to the houses on the other side, then directly to her left and right. If anyone was watching her, they would see a neighbor stopping by with a small package. Then they would see a neighbor walk to the gate in the fence, discover the gate did not have a lock, then quickly and quietly disappear through the gate into the side yard, which is exactly what she did.

So far there had been nothing and no one to see here. The yard was as unremarkable as the house. Maggie walked along the side, too low now to see in the first floor windows. She looked down, and was suddenly curious: the basements windows were boarded up. They were small and encased in window wells. Approaching one of them, she realized the wood was new. The windows had been sealed up recently.

Strange, Maggie thought. *Why would he board up the windows now?*

Is this what Alice saw? she wondered. Was Checks part of this, or had Alice simply gone exploring where she was not wanted, looking for her runaway cat?

It was only after she'd walked along the side of the house, staring down at the boarded up windows, that she turned into the back yard and saw it: a cellar door, the kind few houses had anymore, raised slightly in a 30-degree angle from the ground. One of the door's two sides was thrown back, and as Maggie approached it, she could see stairs leading down into darkness.

Maybe he has an alarm system on the upstairs, she thought, surprised Davies would leave an entry to his house opened and exposed. Or maybe, like Maggie very recently, he simply didn't think anyone would ever break into his house.

Until Alice.

She had to keep reminding herself of the seriousness of the situation.

She stood just outside the cellar door looking down.

After a moment, she called out, "Is anyone home? It's Maggie Dahl. Hello?"

Getting no answer, she debated with herself whether or not to enter the cellar. Then she heard it—a muffled cry, as if someone far off were calling for help.

"Is someone down there?" she called. "Hello?"

The sound came again, more like an animal this time than a human, and Maggie suddenly wondered if this is where Checks had gone that first day.

Steeling herself as best she could, she opened the other half of the cellar door, letting light down into the stairwell. She slipped her hand into her purse, feeling the gun for security, then she headed down into the basement.

The first thing Maggie noticed was the warmth. It struck her as odd. Houses were certainly warm in October, most of them having turned on their heat by now, given winter's slow approach. But basements were always cold. It's what made them the coolest place in a house during summer's high heat. This basement, however, was heated.

She slowly descended, leaving the steps and walking into a completely finished room. It wasn't unusual for people to turn their basements into rec rooms or home offices. Davies had made his quite comfortable: a couch and matching chair, a coffee table, a large screen television on a chest of some kind. And a bed.

A bed? Maggie wondered. That was an odd addition, unless he used it as a guest room—a strange choice for a man who lived alone and was reputed to be a recluse.

She'd been able to see all this in the dim light from outside. Then something caught her eye: a sliver of light seeping out from beneath a closed door in the back of the basement. A staircase leading upstairs was to the left, with the door across from it to Maggie's right. There was another room down here. Was it another furnished room? A wine cellar perhaps? Although having a heated basement would make it ineffective for storing wine.

She reached the door and was surprised to see a padlock on it, open and hanging loose. She stared at the lock, trying to make sense of it all: a heated basement, a door with a light on behind it, a padlock left open and hanging.

Just open the door, Maggie, she told herself.

She felt her resolve weaken. What was there to be afraid of? Why was she reacting this way?

She reached out and removed the padlock. She opened the door, pulled it back, and gasped at what she saw.

Inside the room was a large cage. It contained a desk, a dresser, a bed, and a woman.

Already knowing the answer, Maggie said to the woman, "You're Lilly Stapley, aren't you?"

The woman sat in a small child's rocking chair, too big for it but oblivious to that fact. She stared up at Maggie, both understanding her and uncomprehending of what was happening. It was, Maggie believed, the inevitable result of being confined in a basement cage for ten years.

"He took you, didn't he? It was Cal Davies."

The whistling provided her answer. That same vaguely familiar but unidentifiable tune, blown quietly through the pursed lips of a killer.

"I see you found the cellar door," Davies said. "I left it open hoping you would. You're very smart, Maggie Dahl. Too smart for your own good, but I think you know that by now."

Maggie turned around and saw Davies standing at the bottom of the cellar steps, backlit by the light from outside.

"I brought you something," he said.

Maggie glanced down and saw a claw hammer identical to the one she'd purchased at his store, *indistinguishable but for the blood from the one she'd found by Alice's crushed skull.*

He walked toward her and stopped. Not ready to

come in for the kill, wanting, she assumed, to educate her before he bludgeoned her.

"I'd never boarded up the basement windows," Cal said, explaining the circumstances he must have known she wondered about. "I didn't see any need to. The house is alarmed, as well as equipped with surveillance cameras discreetly placed around the property so I can see what's going on.

Alice must have thought her cat was in my house. I don't know why. She was a strange and annoying woman. But she found one of the basement windows unlocked—even I make mistakes after ten years of being undiscovered—and in she crawled. Short, inappropriate, stupid Alice, squeezing through my basement window. Snooping. Breaking the law. Unaware I could see her on a video feed upstairs. And finding my prize, my sweet Lilly, just like you did. Someone should have taught you both about boundaries a long time ago. You're in a place you don't belong and won't be leaving alive."

Maggie let her arm slide casually to her side, placing her hand next to her purse.

"Why would you keep a child in your basement?" Maggie asked, buying time.

"I don't see a child here," Davies said with a smile. "Do you?"

Lilly Stapley remained silent in the cage behind Maggie. Did she even still know how to speak? Maggie wondered. Of course she did. She was twelve when this monster kidnapped her.

Maggie's hand slipped closer to her purse, her fingers prepared to grab the gun grip inside it.

She saw Davies tighten his fist around the hammer.

"I can throw this faster than you can get to your

phone," he said. "By the time you hit 911 you'll have a hammer buried in your forehead."

He stepped toward her. Maggie looked at the stairs behind him, the light from outside, wondering if she could distract him somehow and make an escape into the backyard. She'd never shot a *person* before, only targets at a range. She let her hand fall against her purse.

"I'll just shut the cellar door and give us some privacy."

Davies turned around, intending to close the door behind him … and froze.

Chip McGill stood on the last step into the basement, silhouetted by light from the stairs.

"You destroyed my life," Chip said. "I've come to return the favor."

Cal Davies shouted and lunged at Chip, the hammer held high above his head. A moment later the men were struggling on the floor, Chip gripping Davies's wrist in an effort to keep the hammer from being brought down on his face.

Do something, Maggie told herself. *Davies is bigger, stronger, enraged. Do something now!*

Without thinking about it, without considering her movements, Maggie pulled the gun from her purse and hurried to the struggling men.

"Drop the hammer or I'll put a bullet in your brain," she said, holding the Glock in both hands and aiming it mere feet from the back of Cal Davies's head.

Her decision had come just in time. Davies had freed his arm and was holding the hammer directly above Chip. If he chose to, he could still bring it smashing into the smaller man's skull.

Knowing the moment was critical, Maggie shouted,

"I mean it, I will shoot you!"

She thrust the gun upward and fired a warning shot.

Did you just do that, seriously? she asked herself. *What if the bullet went through the ceiling and killed someone upstairs? No one's home, idiot, stay focused.*

The door leading to the kitchen burst open, followed by the sound of Sergeant Hoyt rushing down the stairs.

"Don't do it," Hoyt shouted, aiming his service pistol at the man now straddling Chip McGill's chest. "Either I'll kill you, or she will."

Davies calculated his odds. He could still do serious damage to the man who'd taken the blame for his actions a decade ago, the man who, despite being cleared, had always borne the stain and the damage of accusation. But then they would surely both shoot him, one in the front and one in the back.

He was many things. A kidnapper, a murderer, a rapist, a sexual predator extraordinaire … and a coward.

He let the hammer fall to the floor, precariously close to Chip's left temple.

"Now get off him," Hoyt said, stepping further into the room, his gun still aimed at Davies. "Turn around, hands above your head."

Davies did as he was told, climbing off Chip and turning slowly around, clasping his hands in the air.

Hoyt reached into his jacket pocket and pulled out a zip tie.

"You can put the gun away now, Mrs. Dahl," Hoyt said. "We'll talk about your possession of it later. Your sister called me as soon as you left the house."

Of course she did, thought Maggie. *And she'll never let*

me forget it.

Standing behind Davies, Hoyt holstered his gun and quickly used the zip tie to handcuff Davies.

"I thought I was too late," Hoyt said. "I had to break the door down when no one answered."

"We couldn't hear you," replied Maggie. "The basement is soundproofed."

"Soundproofed?"

"Yes. Lilly Stapley is here."

Both Sergeant Hoyt and Chip McGill had been unaware of the room with the open door and the cage beyond it.

Yanking Davies to his feet, Hoyt said, "What are you talking about?"

"She's talking about my accomplishment," Davies said. "See for yourself."

Chip had already rushed to the doorway, peering into the cage and gasping at what he saw. "Oh my God."

"God had nothing to do with it," Davies said.

"Shut up!" Hoyt demanded. "You'll be able to talk all you want in custody."

"I say nothing without a lawyer."

"I don't think the best of them will get you out of this," Maggie said.

The next thing she heard was Sergeant Bryan Hoyt calling for backup, adding to the dispatcher, "We found Lilly Stapley."

That simple declaration was about to explode across the town, through the media and into the world. Whatever private show Cal Davies had enjoyed for ten years would be a global circus by nightfall.

CHAPTER Forty

DAHL HOUSE JAMS AND SPECIALTIES opened on schedule two days after the discovery that sent shock waves through Lambertville and far beyond. Maggie had seen no reason to postpone it, despite being advised by friends and her son to wait.

"What for?" she'd asked Wynn when he'd called from Queens. "Waiting isn't going to change anything. Peter and his daughter will be gone for months, if they ever come back. They've taken her out of state to work with experts. And I promised your father ..."

"Dad's dead, Mom," Wynn had replied, less gently than Maggie would have liked. He'd pressured her to move on from David's death, and even to date men again. She ignored him.

"Then I promised myself," she replied. "There, is that good enough, Wynn? I owe it to me, and to the people who work for me, to make sure this show goes on. We worked so hard for it. No, it's not being postponed. Are you and Leo still coming?"

"That's a crazy question," said Wynn.

He and his boyfriend Leo had made plans weeks ago to stay with Maggie for several nights during the opening. Now that Gerri lived in the house, Maggie intended to give them her room and sleep on the sofa bed in David's study. Maggie had not changed anything in that room and had no immediate plans to. She liked having one room frozen in time where she could sense her husband's presence.

They'd spent an hour on the phone. Maggie had filled Wynn in on life with Aunt Gerri, leaving out details about Tom Brightmore. Wynn had talked about a new job he was hoping to get, and about his and Leo's plans for marriage in the spring. What they had not talked much about was Maggie finding Lilly Stapley in a basement cage, or the media circus that followed, or just how easily she could have been killed. It wasn't too soon to open her store, but it was too soon to talk about the most traumatic event of her life besides finding her husband dead next to her in bed.

Wynn said they'd rent a car and drive, with plans to tour Pennsylvania after a few days and see the fall foliage.

Several of Maggie's friends from Manhattan had come also, taking a bus from Port Authority to Lambertville, where they disembarked at a gas station. The sight of four of her oldest, dearest friends climbing down from a commuter bus had been something to behold. They'd all booked rooms at the Lambertville Station Restaurant and Inn, a luxurious, sprawling complex on the banks of the Delaware River. They had also insisted they were perfectly fine being ignored while Maggie went about the hectic business of opening her store while they enjoyed fine dining and walks across the bridge to New Hope.

There were TV trucks parked outside her house the morning Maggie headed to the store for the big opening. She'd ignored them for two days and intended to continue waving away their questions. She was being portrayed as a hero, the woman who found long lost Lilly Stapley after everyone but her father had given up hope she was alive. This, Maggie knew, was not quite true: Peter Stapley had also assumed his daughter was dead, as had Maggie herself. No one, in fact, expected to see a now-twenty-two-year-old Lilly sitting in a cage in a neighbor's basement.

Maggie also knew no one had more questions than she did. Had Cal Davies built his lair for a captive he hadn't yet abducted? Was it just waiting for Lilly or some other innocent child? Or had he kept them concealed while he built his cage, one bar at a time, all the while serving customers at a hardware store they'd all been going to for years?

The answers would have to wait. For one thing, Cal wasn't talking, barricading himself behind a team of lawyers no doubt as interested in the fame the case would bring them as in any amount of remuneration Cal could provide. For another thing, Lilly herself was gone, whisked away to a clinic in upstate New York that dealt with victims of the kind of trauma Lilly had most assuredly experienced, the details of which Maggie would be happy to never know.

Finally, there was the store opening. It had been six months since David died. He had not lived to see the opening of Dahl House Jams and Specialties, but he would be proud of what Maggie had achieved. She had gone ahead with their vision as much for her husband as for herself. This had all been a couple's dream, not just his or hers. They'd done it all together, and to Maggie's mind, they still were.

Morning bled into afternoon, and afternoon slipped quickly into evening. Everyone was there, including news reporters who were kept outside by one of the off-duty police officers who'd volunteered to help Maggie, "*the* Maggie Dahl," as he'd said when he realized she was the one who'd found the Stapley child. (Oddly, everyone kept thinking of Lilly as a child still, because that's what she'd been when she was last known to be alive. It would take time for the world to know and see the woman Lilly Stapley, if they ever did.)

Maggie allowed herself to enjoy the evening. She'd come so far, so quickly. The people who had helped her were all there in the store, enjoying wine, cheeses and a cello player. ("Seriously, Maggie?" Gerri had teased her. "A *cello* player? What is this, the Met?") Gloria and Sybil kept trying to sell jams, jellies and pottery, despite Maggie having told them this was not a work event. Only Janice was on duty, spending most of her time through the day and night at the cash register. Maggie had decided that morning to offer her a stake in the business. Not a raise—she couldn't afford that at this point—but a piece of a pie she believed would grow over time.

Peter Stapley was off with his daughter, as he should be. His ex-wife Melissa was rumored to have flown to meet them in New York. It was another detail they may never know, and that was up to Peter to reveal if he chose to.

Maggie stood by the cash register taking it all in. Her Manhattan friends were gathered in a clique in one corner, her son Wynn and his now-fiancé Leo were standing in another, lost in conversation.

"A penny for your thoughts."

Startled, Maggie turned to see Sergeant Bryan Hoyt standing next to her, a glass of wine in his hand.

"Where's your wife?" Maggie asked, looking around to see if she could guess who that might be.

"Jennifer's at home," he replied. "With the baby."

Maggie felt foolish. She had known so little about the man who helped save her life, and she had not wondered about him. She'd been so caught up in her own fixations that she hadn't even considered he *had* a life. Not only did he have one, but he had a baby at home.

"I'm so sorry," Maggie said, blushing.

"For what, Maggie? I think I can call you that now. There's nothing for you to be sorry about. I told you, I don't mix business with pleasure, and I don't discuss my personal life with strangers. And let's face it, until about forty-eight hours ago you were both a stranger and a suspect."

"That sounds like business," Maggie said, glancing at his wine glass.

"All right, well, I almost never mix the two. But the lines are pretty blurred here, aren't they? Anyway, congratulations, and we still need to discuss that gun you have."

"It's licensed!" Maggie said. "It belonged to my husband. Please don't—"

"Don't worry, I'm playing with you. But we have to discuss it. The defense will bring it up in court for one reason or another."

The defense. It reminded Maggie that this was not over. There would be a trial, assuming Cal Davies did not accept a plea deal. It could go on for months, and Maggie would find herself as a witness in a courtroom … a long time from now. It wasn't something to allow into her thoughts tonight, and she wouldn't.

"Tell Jennifer I hope to meet her soon," Maggie said. "And the baby."

"I'll do that," Hoyt replied. He raised his glass to

her, then turned and walked away.

No sooner had Hoyt left, than Gerri walked in with Tom Brightmore. Maggie had told Gerri to enjoy herself, she wasn't needed or expected at the store. The opening, yes, but only when she got there. And now she had. She'd arrived well into the evening, and she'd shown up with her arm laced around Tom's. If this was not dating, Maggie didn't know what was.

One more look around, old girl, she told herself. She would spend the rest of the night schmoozing, chatting, and maybe even selling a jam jar or two. She would catch up with Gerri and the man she swore would not be her fourth husband, despite indications to the contrary. She would thank Gloria, Sybil and Janice for all they'd done at least three more times, asking Janice to meet her for breakfast, there was something she wanted to talk about.

And finally, as midnight neared and everyone had gone home, she would crawl into bed with Checks on the pillow and David in her heart. If she dreamed at all, she hoped it would be a good one. A "Well done, my love," from David, perhaps with a satisfied cat somewhere in the corner.

For tonight, she knew, she would sleep soundly.

UP NEXT: Open Secrets: A Maggie Dahl Mystery

It's been six months since the opening of Dahl House Jams and Specialties. The shop is humming and Maggie is turning a profit, securing her place as a stable merchant among the shops of Lambertville.

Sister Gerri has planted herself firmly in Maggie's world and in her house, showing no signs of finding her own place while she pursues a relationship with Tom Brightmore.

The factory has expanded, adding three new employees even as they've said goodbye to Peter Stapley, who has finally left the town where his pain had festered and deepened for ten years. What lies ahead for Peter and his family we may never know.

Meanwhile, local author Shanna Delaney has made the most of her limited fame, selling her book of essays about life in Lambertville and the Delaware River Valley in every local shop that will have it. She's had two readings at Booketeria, the town's bookstore, and made trips to Philadelphia and New York City for book signings.

Maggie often sees her at the coffee shop with her laptop, writing a follow up collection. It seems Shanna has decided go from writing about life in the town, to writing about its people. Then, one beautiful day in May, Shanna isn't there. Nor is she there the next day, or the next. It seems Shanna Delany has gone missing, while leaving behind everything she owned.

Maggie knows that no one ever really vanishes into thin air. With Gerri even more firmly by her side, she decides to find out what happened to Shanna Delaney.

Into that thin air they walk, surrounded by mist and mystery as they seek to uncover what stories Shanna had been telling with her laptop and her morning coffee, and who did not want them told.

A NOTE FROM MARK

Thank you for taking a ride on the mystery train. I hope you've enjoyed the scenery and the company. If you have a moment to write a review that would be much appreciated. Even a few sentences help other readers discover the books and meet the characters.

You can find me at my website, MarkMcNease.com, and also on Twitter (@MyMadeMark), Facebook (MarkMcNeaseWriter) and Goodreads. I'm always happy to hear directly from readers as well, and I answer every email, so don't be shy, drop me a note anytime (Mark@MarkMcNease.com).

Writing is both my passion and my pleasure, and by the time you read this I'll be working on the next story ... and the next.

Yours from the thickening plot,

Mark

92686202R00143

Made in the USA
Lexington, KY
08 July 2018